Samuel French Acting Edition

The Faculty Room

by Bridget Carpenter

FOR PRODUCTION ENQUIRIES

UNITED STATES AND CANADA
info@concordtheatricals.com
1-866-979-0447

UNITED KINGDOM AND EUROPE
licensing@concordtheatricals.co.uk
020-7054-7200

Each title is subject to availability from Concord Theatricals, depending
upon country of performance. Please be aware that *THE FACULTY
ROOM* may not be licensed by Concord Theatricals in your territory.
Professional and amateur producers should contact the nearest
Concord Theatricals office or licensing partner to verify availability.

For all enquiries regarding motion picture, television, and other media rights, please contact Concord Theatricals.

MUSIC USE NOTE

IMPORTANT BILLING AND CREDIT REQUIREMENTS

Originally commissioned by Atlantic Theatre Company.
World premiere in the 2003 Humana Festival of New American Plays
at Actors Theatre of Louisville.

actors theatre of louisville **PRESENTS**
27th Annual Humana Festival of New American Plays
made possible by a generous grant from The Humana Foundation

The Faculty Room

march **11** - april **05, 2003**

by **BRIDGET CARPENTER**
directed by **SUSAN FENICHELL**

THE CAST (in order of appearance)

Carver	**GREG McFADDEN***
Zoe	**REBECCA WISOCKY***
Adam	**MICHAEL LAURENCE***
Principal Dennis	**COLIN McPHILLAMY***
Bill	**WILLIAM McNULTY***
Student	**JOHN CATRON†**

Setting: An ugly small suburb in an ugly small city somewhere in the middle of the United States of America. The faculty lounge of a public school: Madison-Feurey High School. The time is the present.

Scenic Designer	**PAUL OWEN**
Costume Designer	**LORRAINE VENBERG**
Lighting Designer	**MARY LOUISE GEIGER**
Sound Designer/Original Music	**SHANE RETTIG**
Properties Designer	**APRIL HARTSOOK**
Stage Manager	**LESLIE K. OBERHAUSEN***
Assistant Stage Manager	**ANDREW SCHEER***
Fight Director	**BRENT LANGDON**
Dramaturg	**AMY WEGENER**
Casting	**JERRY BEAVER**
Directing Assistant	**EMILY WRIGHT**
High School Anthem by	**CHRIS HARRISON**

*Member of Actors' Equity Association, the union of professional actors and stage managers of the United States
† Member of Actors Theatre's Apprentice Company

Presented by special arrangement with Helen Merrill Ltd.
Originally commissioned by Atlantic Theater Company
New York, NY

Woolly Mammoth Theatre Company

Howard Shalwitz   **Kevin Moore**
Artistic Director   *Managing Director*

presents

The Faculty
R om

by Bridget Carpenter
directed by Howard Shalwitz

June 5 - July 9, 2006

Cast (in order of appearance)
Carver Durand...Michael Russotto*
Zoe Bartholemew...Megan Anderson*
Principal Dennis...Michael Willis*
Adam Younger...Ethan T. Bowen*
Bill Dunn...Michael Willis*
Student...Miles Butler

Production
Set Design...Robin Stapley
Lighting Design...Jay A. Herzog
Sound Design...Michael Kraskin
Costume Design...Melanie Clark
Properties...Jennifer Sheetz
Fight Choreography...John Gurski
Production Stage Manager...William V. Carlton*

*Member, Actors' Equity Association

PLACE:
An ugly small suburb in an ugly
small town somewhere in the middle
of the United States of America.

SETTING:
The faculty lounge of a public
school, Madison-Feurey High.

This performance has one
15-minute intermission

Produced with special permission by Olivia
Wingate Productions. Originally commissioned
by Atlantic Theatre Company. World premiere
in the 2003 Humana Festival of New American
Plays at Actors Theatre of Louisville.

CHARACTERS

ZOE BARTHOLEMHEW (teaches Theater) – About 30 years old

ADAM YOUNGER (teaches English) – About 40 years old

CARVER DURAND (teaches World History [temporary regional certification]) – About 30 years old

BILL (teaches Ethics) – Somewhere between 40 and death.

PRINCIPAL DENNIS (a voice on the P.A. System)

A STUDENT (male, freshman)

Zoe, Adam, and Carver are attractive; not particularly healthy-looking, though.

TIME

Now

PLACE

An ugly small suburb in an ugly small town somewhere in the middle of the United States of America. It feels like the middle of nowhere. It feels like the center of exactly nothing. It feels like the moon.

SETTING

A faculty lounge of a public school: Madison-Feurey High School.

The lights are flourescent. The floor is linoleum. There are no windows. The walls are some institutional color.

The coffee maker is always, always on.

The couches are drab vinyl.

There is a giant cardinal head from an old mascot costume perched atop a cupboard.

There are ashtrays everywhere, full to overflowing.

Lots of ancient inexplicable teacher shit is tucked in corners, scattered around the room.

It's a halfway place that smells like stale smoke and mimeograph ink.

Just like in casinos, in the faculty room, it's impossible to tell what time it is.

NOTE – The Madison-Feurey School Anthem (scene. 2) has music composed by Chris Harrison. For information and to obtain the music, please contact author's agent. at Creative Artists Agency, 2000 Avenue of the Stars, Los Angeles, CA 90067 Attn: Renee Kurtz.

ACTING NOTES

Talk fast, always. Jump cues.
Don't be afraid to be mean or make a joke at another character's expense.
Lean into confrontation.
When in doubt, be loud.

THE FACULTY ROOM might be performed without an intermission.
If there is an intermission, it should happen after scene four.

Scene One

SEPTEMBER

CARVER grades papers at the table of the faculty room, a pile of books beside him. He appears somewhat ill at ease. CARVER is clean-cut, organized, anxious, and full to bursting with big ideas.

ZOE enters, slamming the door. ZOE is disheveled in a sexy way that suggests she does it on purpose. Burnout well underway, ZOE's hard to fool.

She doesn't acknowledge CARVER. Instead she dumps her once-chic bag on the ground, rummaging through it with some urgency.

CARVER looks at her. Now that she's entered, he seems even more awkward.

CARVER. *(clearing throat)* Morning.

(ZOE keeps rummaging.)

CARVER. Morning.

ZOE looks up. She stares at him in silence for a longer-than-comfortable moment. She goes back to her bag.

CARVER, *bewildered, returns to grading.*

ZOE. *(intense pleasure)* Oh yes.

She lights a cigarette, inhales, and leans back on the hard vinyl couch, holding in her smoke.

Over the couch a handwritten sign has been taped to the wall. It reads NO SMOKING PLEASE!!!!

P.A. SYSTEM *clicks on:*
[elephant trumpet]

Click: P.A. SYSTEM off. Click on again.

P.A. SYSTEM. Uh…Morning announcements will begin in a few minutes.

[elephant trumpet]

Click: **P.A. SYSTEM** *off.*

ADAM *barrels in, kicking the door open with his foot; it slams behind him. Handsome, unkempt, magnetic, and 40ish,* **ADAM** *has the energy of a pressure cooker. The potential to blow is always there. When he tells a story, words come out of his mouth like water from a fire hose. His mood swings are extreme and instantaneous.*

He holds 3 or 4 variously-sized handguns and unceremoniously dumps them on the counter.

ADAM. *(a grand pronouncement)* I Hate Morning Checkpoints!

ADAM *methodically checks each gun to see if it's loaded. After checking each one, he opens up a chute in the wall [not unlike a postal-box unit] and tosses in the unloaded guns.*

He sees **ZOE** *smoking.*

ADAM. Gimme gimme you fucking greedy fucking cunt.

She hands **ADAM** *the cigarettes. He fires up with enormous pleasure, holding in smoke. They sit and smoke, paying no attention at all to* **CARVER**, *who sneaks glances at them.*

ADAM. *[long drag; exhale]*
Mother*fuck.*

Little pause.

ZOE. Yeah.

ADAM. Today at checkpoints I began talking with Janet Lundquist and Beth Fisher, both of whom are in my third period Lit class. They said they wanted to talk to me about a book they were both reading. Actually a *series* of books. I nearly fell over. My students, wanting to discuss books? I checked their pupils to see if they had been using. No. Then Janet explains: the books they're reading are about the Rapture. You've heard about the Rapture – it's when God calls all of the Christians home: one day they're walking around, shopping at Kmart, the next moment they're sucked up into the sky, inhaled by the breath of God, only he doesn't eat them, he deposits them gently in Heaven where they stay blissfully for eternity talking about whatever Christians talk about. But the books the girls are reading only mention the Rapture in passing. This series of books is about the people left behind. It's called "Sudden Awakening." Because you and me, Zoe, we're gonna be the infidels left here right smack in the middle of this grand country, all this flat blue sky and flat gray land around us like it is every morning we wake up, when the Rapture comes, it'll be just the same as it is every morning except for, you know, no Christians. More parking spaces. Suddenly awake, us.

And Janet and Beth, they're both near tears – not because they're afraid of the Rapture, no, they're both looking forward to the Rapture, as long as it happens *after* the Christmas formal – but they're weepy because they're worried that some of their less than holy friends might not make it up to Heaven, and then they're going to be up there, and their friends will be down here. And then what would happen?

ZOE. So you comforted them.

ADAM. I comforted them, I did, yes, I pointed out that perhaps there was a divine Guest List, a Guest List for the Rapture made out by none other than God himself, and that people who attend parties do not question why the host or hostess invited who he or she invited, that it was discretionary, and that Beth and Janet should perhaps consider that the number of people invited to the Rapture was in fact the will of God. And then I told them that I thought they could write about "Sudden Awakening" for English class, and they could speculate about who was called to the Rapture and why.

ZOE. Brilliant.

ADAM. You say that with an ironic edge, Zoe, but you know
what? It *is* brilliant, it's brilliant because I am taking life
information, basic life information and I am *crafting* it
into an *assignment:* something easily digested, something
accomplishable, something that provides a concrete
product at its conclusion. Sooner or later Beth Fisher
and Janet Lundquist and Josh Lathe and Daniel Hern-
don and Jin-He Tamako and Sterling Mills and Theresa
Sorkin and Damon Fitzpatrick and Liza Corrado and
Bernardo Lorne and Sandrine Chin and Theodore
Malden and Ashley Richardson and Jesus Rodriguez and
countless other students are going to have to realize that
everything has an assignment embedded in it, life is just
one assignment after the next, and I am doing them a
favor by isolating each assignment and grading it appro-
priately and writing down the results.

ZOE. Beth Fisher wears a W.W.J.D. bracelet.

ADAM. W.W.J.D.

ZOE. What Would Jesus Do.

ADAM *smokes thoughtfully.*

ADAM. Jesus would take off the bracelet, to start, because
bracelets are faggotty.
Haven't seen much of you this week.
So where've you been.

ZOE. I don't know, Adam. Around.

ADAM. You got yourself somebody yet?

ZOE. Maybe I do and maybe I don't.

ADAM. Maybe I do, too.

ZOE. Whatever.

ADAM. How was your...the rest of your summer.

ZOE. It was decent.

ADAM. "Decent."

ZOE. I bought a raft at Kmart and every afternoon I drove
to the St. Jude River and floated in the murky water
and waited for September to come. Now it's here.
That was my summer.

ADAM. I taught summer school. Driver's ed.

ZOE. You told me.

Silence.

ADAM. Fixed up your classroom?

ZOE. Got the girls to do it. They love making collages. Give
'em exacto knives, it's like crack, they're in heaven.

ADAM *widens his eyes at* ZOE.

ADAM. Hello!

*He points to a sign on the wall that has a picture of an
exacto knife with a red circle over it and the word, "NO!"
underneath.*

ADAM. Jay Pasolenski? Lost half an ear last year. Exacto
casualty.

ZOE *stares at* ADAM *with some animosity.*

ZOE. You're not wearing your Exacto-badge. Are you going
to make a citizen's arrest?

ADAM. I'd just hate to see you get in trouble for breaking
the rules, Zoe.

ZOE. Yeah, I know how you love rules.

ADAM. Who are your little helpers?

ZOE. Last year's junior prom court. Marissa Dade, Polly
Kamin, Annie-Kay Phillips, Cherry Duncan, Jessica
Herbert.

CARVER *gets up to fix himself a cup of brackish coffee.
He opens and shuts cupboards and drawers.*

ADAM. What's he doing?

ZOE. I imagine looking for a spoon.

ADAM. Doesn't he know we don't believe in spoons here?

ZOE. Don't know what he believes.

ADAM. He's in for a disappointment when he understands
the dearth of amenities.

ZOE. He'll have to learn to stir the non-dairy creamer with
a bic, like everyone else.

ADAM. Is he grading already? Did he give a quiz the *first week?*

CARVER. He hears.

> **ADAM** *and* **ZOE** *look at him blankly for a moment, then continue talking as though there has been no interruption.*

ADAM.	**CARVER.**
Have I mentioned that as of this month I get up early before school to "work out." It was either that, or gain forty pounds like that tub of lard Coach Salata who, incidentally, told me that he'd like to take you out and quote give you the time unquote.	Man. Forget it.

> **CARVER** *goes back to grading, irritated.*

ZOE. You "work out."

ADAM. I joined Mega-Fitness.

ZOE. ...Mega-shithole.

ADAM. Yeah, but it's a manly mega-shithole. Me and other mega-men are there, grunting, communicating without language, it's a mega-communication. We share a common understanding, we mega-bond. Shit, I forgot to lock my car!

> **ADAM** *runs out.*

> **CARVER** *puts his coffee down loudly.*

CARVER. Can I ask you a question? How come don't you talk to me?

> *A beat.*

ZOE. You spilled on your papers.

CARVER. Oh dammit...

> *He looks for something to wipe up with.*

ZOE. *(re: his search)* Good luck.
> Here.

> *She uses one of her papers to wipe.*

CARVER. Thank you.
> But – that's a paper of your stu–

ZOE. I'll give her a B.

CARVER. Why don't you – why doesn't anyone talk to me? This is just, just bizarre. I mean, I, I meet the principal on the day before classes, he thanks me for accepting the position on such short notice, he shakes my hand, I haven't seen him since. Nobody says hello! Nobody talks to me!

Little pause.

ZOE. You're new.

CARVER. So?

ZOE. That's how it is.

CARVER. Weren't you a new teacher once upon a time?

ZOE. Yes.

CARVER. And?

ZOE. No one talked to me.
...You get used to it.

CARVER. Where is Principal Dennis? He's disappeared.

ZOE. He doesn't like to leave the office. Don't talk about him in here, anyway–

CARVER. *(scoffing)* Why? It's bugged? I mean, this place is about a thousand miles from anything resembling a metropolitan area...

ZOE. Just don't. I'm trying to give you a tip.

(P.A SYSTEM clicks on.)

P.A SYSTEM. *[trumpet flourish]*
[static]
Good morning, everyone.
This is Your Principal, Mr. Dennis.
I'll just wait for everyone to get settled.
I'm still waiting.

Well.	**CARVER.** *(overlapping)*
I trust that you're all having a wonderful first week back at Madison-Feurey High.	I also don't get–

ZOE *shushes* **CARVER**.

She writes on the dry-erase board in large letters:
HE CAN HEAR YOU.

P.A. SYSTEM.

I see a number of familiar faces, as well as faces that are new to me, but that will soon become familiar…

CARVER.

What are you talking about?

*(***ZOE*** puts her finger to her lips: SHHH.)*

(She writes again:
**PA SYSTEM = MICROPHONE
HE HEARS YOU!!***)*

P.A. SYSTEM.
That's what September is all about, recognizing the old, and welcoming the new…

CARVER. *(loud, overlapping)*
Come on, you're kidding. Are you trying to tell me–

(On the PA System, the **PRINCIPAL** *stops for a moment.)*

P.A. SYSTEM. I'll just wait until everyone is listening attentively.

ZOE *gestures: "Told you so."*

P.A. SYSTEM. That's better.

Some of you may have been listening to announcements and wondering, What The Heck are all those noises? For example, the noise you heard a moment ago.

[trumpet flourish]

Well, Principal Dennis is here to tell you. On a recent sweltering afternoon in August, myself, the school board, and some dedicated members of the Madison-Feurey PTA decided in a Unanimous Vote to implement a change in format to our beloved P.A. System. This year, we will be using a variety of *new sounds* to denote the end of a class period. It's a new format, so we'll be giving lots of new noises a try! What an adventure! I'll be listening both to the new P.A. noises and to *your* noises…that, is, your *feedback*, ha ha. Let Principal Dennis know which sounds work for *you*. Remember, Madison-Feurey High is not just a place for *teaching*, but a place for *education*.

[trumpet flourish]

[drilling sound]

[lion roar]

P.A. SYSTEM *clicks off.*

ZOE. Okay, now he's gone.

She glances at a book on **CARVER***'s pile.*

ZOE. What is this? "365 Meditations for Teachers?" You're gay aren't you.

CARVER. What kind of a person are – I mean, you haven't bothered to tell me your name, you talk around me like I'm some piece of furniture –

ZOE. I'm Zoe Bartholemhew. I teach theater. And speech.

CARVER. *(grudging)* Carver. Durand.

ZOE. Hi, Carver. Gay, right?

CARVER. Jesus Christ. Yes. You going to get me fired now? God. I really *need* this job, I moved here from the city to get it because there was nothing, nothing to be found–

ZOE. Last I checked, people didn't get *fired* for being gay.

CARVER. You don't read much, do you.

ZOE. That's funny! You *are* gay. Witty.

CARVER. That's offensive.

ZOE. Boo Hoo. Big deal. I said you were witty, I didn't call you Mary.

CARVER. Unbelievable.

ZOE. Or, ah, "dicksmoker."

CARVER. Thanks for the sensitivity.

ZOE. You're not from here.

CARVER. No.

And you, you're from…

ZOE. Here.

CARVER. Oh.

ZOE. I went here. For high school. This is my alma mater.

CARVER. Really.

ZOE. Adam went here too. And now we both teach here.

CARVER. Huh.

ZOE. "Huh." Surprised?

CARVER. Oh no it's just, uh–

ZOE. So small and ugly?

CARVER. No.

ZOE. A burnt-out strip mall with a few side streets?

CARVER. I'm sure it has its charms. Someplace. I don't know the area too well yet.

ZOE. Pretty much you drive past Beef Barn, Ye Olde Taco Shoppe, and the Used Tire Village, and you've seen the heart of town.

CARVER. Oh.

ZOE. You're from the city?

CARVER. Yes.

ZOE. I've never been.

CARVER. Oh. It's–

ZOE. Don't tell me. I like to imagine. I don't want you to ruin it.

CARVER. All right.

ZOE. Did Principal Dennis put you in charge of Spirit Days?

CARVER. Yes, How did you–

ZOE. He gives every wide-eyed wonder Spirit Days. Word to the wise: ignore it.

CARVER. Oh, I don't mind, I actually have some ideas for a kind of–

ZOE. And as for your sophomore advisees, make them *sign up* for office hours. If you do walk-ins, you'll never see any of them again and we're required by law to have them scheduled so keep records.

CARVER. I, uh, actually met one of my advisees already.

ZOE. Aren't you a champ.

CARVER. In fact I wanted to talk to somebody about uh… the meeting was, well, it was strange. She was strange. A strange girl.

ZOE. Of course she's strange, she's a sophomore. What's her name?

CARVER. Darby Weider.

ZOE. I don't know that name – oh wait does she not wear shoes?

CARVER. Yes.

ZOE. Sure, Darby. Madison-Feury's own little hippie. She was homeschooled until just last year. Lucky you.

    ADAM *enters jubilantly.*

ADAM. I caught a freshman smoking *outside* of a designated smoking area and he had a FULL pack of Marlboros and Guess Who confiscated them! Oh LOOK – did Zoe make a new friend?

ZOE. That's Carver. He teaches – what are you, Biology?

CARVER. World History.

ZOE. Adam teaches English. Carver, Adam; Adam, Carver.

    ADAM *fires up a Marlboro.*

CARVER. I don't know why you haven't talked with me, our classrooms are right on the same hall.

ADAM. Well, see, I hate everybody who's on that hall.

ZOE. *(clarifying)* You hate everybody.

ADAM. I do. I do. – Well, I don't hate Zoe, I'm actually in love with her – profound, besotted love – but as it turns out she doesn't love me and perhaps never will. But I still carry the torch. So there's that.

ZOE. It is so boring when you go into that.

ADAM. Boring doesn't make it a lie, Sweetheart.

That's Zoe's worst insult, Carver. F.Y.I. I've never seen her upset. The only way she registers irritation or frustration or impatience is to call something "a bore."

Now I bet you're in charge of Spirit Days, huh?

BILL *enters;* **ADAM** *stops talking.*

BILL *is a teacher who wears a perpetually blank expression. He sets his briefcase down on the table, takes a personal mug out of the case, pours a cup of coffee, drinks it, rinses and dries the cup, and replaces it in his briefcase. He opens the refrigerator, bends down, and stares inside with great intensity. He stays in this position a long time. The effect should be as though he has frozen there.* **ADAM, CARVER,** *and* **ZOE** *watch him avidly.*

ADAM. HI, BILL!

BILL *has no response, but* **CARVER** *and* **ZOE** *jump at* **ADAM**'s *shout.*

After an eternity, **BILL** *straightens up, closes the refrigerator door, picks up his briefcase, and exits.* **ZOE & ADAM** *smoke, unconcerned.*

CARVER. Does he teach here?

ZOE. Oh, sure, Bill. Bill Dunn. He teaches Ethics.

ADAM. Never heard him utter a syllable.

CARVER. How long have *you* taught here?

ADAM. Forever, baby.

CARVER. I heard you went to school here.

ADAM. *(a quick glance at* **ZOE***)* You hear all kinds of things these days.

CARVER. *(to* **ZOE***)* How about you. How long have you been a teacher?

ZOE. Not as long as Adam. *(to* **ADAM***)* Carver lived in the city.

ADAM. *(registering* **ZOE**'s *interest)* And he came all the way out here to our little patch of paradise to teach with us. How senseless and fascinating. Where exactly were you teaching in the city?

CARVER. Oh, uh, a couple of places, here and there.

ADAM. Well go ahead and name one, my curiosity's piqued.

*(***P.A. SYSTEM*** clicks on.)*

P.A. SYSTEM. *[organ chord]*
  Second period will begin in ten minutes. Thank you.
  [horse gallop]

  (Click: **P.A. SYSTEM** *off.)*

ADAM. Where were we?

CARVER. ...I should get to class. It was...nice...to talk to
  you both. See you later.

ADAM. Have you picked a girlfriend yet?

CARVER. Excuse me?

ADAM. Picked a girlfriend.

  Pause.

CARVER. I don't. Ah. That's not – I'm sure I'm misunderst
  ... what, what do you mean.

ADAM. A Girlfriend. From Your Classes.

CARVER. Don't be silly that's a ridiculous statement you
  have to be kidding.

ADAM. Are you all right, Carver? You seem not all right.

CARVER. You're talking about "picking girlfriends" – that's
  not funny.

ADAM. Zoe's picked. Usually I haven't picked a girlfriend
  by this time – I tend to take my time – but Zoe *always*
  has her guy by the end of Freshman Orientation. She's
  got a good eye.

ZOE. Flatterer.

  Little pause.

CARVER. This is a kind of hazing ritual for new faculty, I
  assume. Right? First you don't talk to me, then you ask
  me to tell you that I'm dating a *minor*.

  Little pause.

ADAM. You're sort of a drag, aren't you, Carver?

ZOE. He seems like it, but he's gay! Funny!

ADAM. Ohhh.
  So have you picked a *boy*friend yet.

CARVER. Whatever it is you're implying, I don't get it, and I don't think it's funny.

ADAM. Which is it? Can't be both. If you don't get it, that's one thing, but if that's true, it's not logical that you don't think it's funny, because how can you decide it's *unfunny* if you don't get it?

CARVER. You pick.

ADAM. Carver, I'm sharing! I'm asking questions of a fellow teacher, I'm trying to tell you something personal, something about my life as a *longtime* faculty member at Madison-Feurey High.

ZOE. *(to ADAM)* And why is that.

ADAM. I just want to get to know our new friend.

CARVER *goes along with the joke.*

CARVER. Okay. Fine. So who's your boyfriend?

ZOE. Raphael Gilberto.

ADAM. Is that so!

ZOE. Yeah.

ADAM. You're sure.

ZOE. You bet I'm sure. Raphael.

ADAM. Well. *(to CARVER)* She goes for the sensitive types. Last year Raphael was voted "Still Waters Run Deep."

CARVER. *(laughing)* You guys are pretty funny.

ADAM. What's funny? How come you're not asking who my girlfriend's gonna be?

CARVER. I'm sure you'll tell me whether I ask or not.

ADAM. My girlfriend is going to be Jen Carlson.

ZOE. You're kidding.

ADAM. Have you seen her class picture yet? They just came back, and she gave me one.

ZOE. She takes a nice picture.

ADAM. Don't be jealous, Zoe, it's so unattractive on a woman your age. I don't know that you ever took quite so delectable a picture. Look at her. Look at that skin. That is the picture you see in the dictionary next to the entry "peaches and cream." – Jen was voted Best Complexion. I asked her what her favorite foods were, and she said: pizza, rice cakes with peanut butter and honey, and Twix. I don't mind admitting it, I think I'm in love.

ZOE. That's too bad.

ADAM. Why's that.

ZOE. Polly told me this morning that Jen Carlson was in love with my Raphael.

ADAM. Bullshit.

ZOE. Adam, Polly Kamin is Jen's best friend. Polly *always* knows what's going on. You know that.

ADAM *looks grumpy. He does know that.*

ZOE. Poor Jen.
Guess you'll have to find another girlfriend.

ADAM. I'm not finding another girlfriend, Zoe. You know the rules.

ZOE *shrugs.*

ADAM. Besides. This just makes things interesting.

ZOE. What's that supposed to mean?

ADAM. We'll have an interesting year.
Look at him.

ZOE. Poor Carver.

ADAM. Thinks we're serious!

They laugh.

ZOE. Well, we are serious.

A moment.

CARVER. You two are very strange.

ADAM. You should have seen us when we were married.

Blackout.

Scene Two

OCTOBER

CARVER wears a Halloween costume. He's a ghost [so actually we can't tell it's Carver] and he wears a sheet with two holes cut out for eyes.

He stands in front of a portable keyboard which sits on the table, wearing headphones, picking at the keys, rocking out a little bit.

ZOE enters. She wears a witch costume. She carries a handgun and a rifle. As she speaks, she checks each gun to see if it's loaded [neither are] then dumps the guns down the chute.

ZOE. That little Carrie Mulligan thinks she's such a smart-ass. I told her I'd check her purse, it's routine, and she insists it's too small to hold anything, it's all part of her costume (she says she's a hooker but I couldn't tell the difference between what she was wearing and what she usually wears) and lo and behold, when I open the purse, she's packing. It's ridiculous. They think just because it's Halloween I'm not going to *check*. Buddy Cummings came to school dressed as a cowboy, and he thinks he gets to carry a rifle around all day!? Think again.

CARVER is still picking at the keyboard.

ZOE. Carver? Happy Halloween.

She takes off his headphones which he wears outside of the sheet.

ZOE. Boo!

CARVER screams, recovers himself.

CARVER. Zoe, hi, I'm glad you're early, I need your help.

ADAM enters in a priest's cassock, carrying a rosary. He makes the sign of the cross. He holds up a "Sudden Awakening" novel like it's the Bible.

ADAM. *(perhaps an Irish priest's intonation)* Hello my children. We are all of us sinners. Yet we can be redeemed if we confess. Listen: "Immediately after the tribulation of those days" – that means after the rapture – "the sun shall be darkened, and the moon shall not give her light, and the stars shall fall from heaven." That's the epigraph for chapter four of "Sudden Awakening" *(gloating)* My first assignment of the year has woken sleeping giants.

CARVER. Adam, hi, good, I need you, too.

ADAM. All of us "need" each other, my son.

CARVER. I was digging around some old files in the storage room…

ADAM. Why?!

CARVER. No reason, anyway I found the Madison-Feurey school anthem! I bet you didn't even know we had an anthem. So last night I pulled out my Yamaha to fool around with the tune a little bit, and I made a new arrangement! So listen, you guys, I want you to help me out at assembly. We can teach it to everyone! I printed out the melody, it's very simple, you guys can look at the sheet music and follow along…

ZOE. Mrs. Lund is going to be mad.

CARVER. All she cares about is the Spring Sing! She doesn't care about the anthem!

ZOE. It's your funeral.

CARVER. OK, I know everyone thinks they know the best way to do things, but indulge me and try this one idea.

ZOE. I have a soft spot for you because you're a fag stuck here, of all places. But suddenly – showtunes? For school? It's asking too much.

CARVER. It's not "The Rose." It's a school song!

ZOE. Are you trying to win some kind of McDonald's teaching award, Carver? Because we're not even on the radar. Your anthem is just a penny in a well. No one can read ABC, let alone music.

CARVER. Everybody can sing something. It's just for school spirit. Getting ready for spirit days!

ADAM. Spirit Days aren't until March.

CARVER. So we have time to re-imagine the anthem!

ADAM lights a cigarette thoughtfully.

ADAM. "Spirit days." Vodoun.

The dead, resurrected from the earth.

ZOE. They *are* zombies.

ADAM. *(singsong) Libera me, Domine, de morte aeterna...*

CARVER. Don't give up. You're giving up.

ADAM, smoking, makes the sign of the cross at him.

ADAM. *(singsong) Requiem aeternam dona eis.*

CARVER. You think that's pretty clever, huh.

ADAM. I actually do. It's Latin.

ADAM smokes.

CARVER. Goddammit. Goddammit. You're gone. You both gave up before I got here; before I knew anything about this godforsaken school, you had already begun and completed the process of total detachment. The thing that's scariest about you two, you don't look the part. You're employed, you bathe, *(to ZOE)* you direct scenes from *Cat on a Hot Tin Roof, (to ADAM)* you read Salinger out loud, you show up more or less on time, you carry on conversations – not normal conversations, but still – and you *maintain* the *illusion* that you participate. But you don't believe in anything, and you think it makes you safe – but it makes you small. YOUR WHOLE LIFE IS A SHRUG. THERE'S NOTHING THERE, NO STANDARDS, NO MORALS, NO BOUNDARIES! BECAUSE *YOU HAVE GIVEN UP!* QUITTERS! ZOMBIES! *THEY'RE* NOT THE DEAD ONES, YOU ARE! *YOU'RE* NOT A WITCH, AND *YOU'RE* NOT A PRIEST, YOU'RE BOTH *ZOMBIES!* ZOMBIES! ZOMBIES!

Little pause.

ADAM. Damn, Carver, I'll learn the song.

ZOE. I'll learn it, too, okay, calm down.

CARVER. I just want to teach you my version of the fucking school anthem!

ZOE. We said we'd learn it!

CARVER. Okay, great. *(to* **ZOE***)* Can you follow harmony?

ZOE. I guess.

They pick up the sheet music.

CARVER. I programmed the arrangement into my keyboard memory last night, so I just have to push a button. Okay, ready?

ADAM/ZOE. Yeah.

> **CARVER** *pushes a button on the keyboard; the anthem begins, and the three of them sing together.*

CARVER/ZOE/ADAM. *(singing)*

OH:
HERE'S TO THE CARDINAL RED AND WHITE
SCHOOL COLORS BRAVE AND TRUE

AT MADISON-FEUREY HIGH
OUR COLORS WON'T CHANGE HUE
TRADITION AND LOYALTY ARE WHAT WE LEARN
HEARTY EDUCATION IS THE BEST RETURN
RALLIES, FOOTBALL, BASKETBALL, AND SPIRIT DAYS
THOSE ARE THE THINGS FOR WHICH WE RAISE OUR SONG
IN PRAISE.

WE WON'T GIVE UP
WE WON'T GIVE IN
WE WON'T GIVE OUT
WE WON'T!

SOOOO HERE'S TO THE CARDINAL RED AND WHITE
NOT BROWN, OR BLACK, OR BLUE

OH MADISON-FEUREY HIGH
WE WILL REMEMBER YOU
YES, WE'LL REMEMBER YOU

Pause. **ADAM** *wipes his eyes.* **ZOE** *clears her throat.*

ADAM. That was really something.

CARVER. You have a good voice.

ADAM. No, I don't – do I?

CARVER. Yeah. You sounded good.

ADAM. That song did something to me. I feel…moved. Your song moved me.

CARVER. I just did the arrangement…the song was already there…

ADAM. And you know what, you might have been right. About giving up. Zoe won't talk about it, but–

ZOE. Shut up.

ADAM. You shut up!

ZOE. No you shut up!

ADAM. I think you're jealous because I have the capacity to be emotionally moved by a song and you don't. You don't possess the capacity to be moved by, by what. Who knows. I mean go ahead, tell me what moves you!

ZOE. First of all, I'm emotionally moved by plenty of things, and secondly, you'd never know, because god knows it's never happened while you're in the room!

ADAM. Carver's right – you've given up!

ZOE. On *you.*

CARVER. Okay, this doesn't have to happen…

ADAM. Who asked you?

ZOE. Yeah, Carver, stay out of it!

CARVER. Jesus! No wonder nobody else comes in here!

ADAM. *(to* **ZOE***)* You're angry because he created something that you have no idea how to respond to!

> **ADAM** *slams out the door.*

CARVER. Is this a…

I guess…maybe I should go get Adam?

> **ZOE** *doesn't answer.*

CARVER. Yeah. I'm going to go find Adam.

> **CARVER** *leaves.*

Door opens. **BILL** *enters. He doesn't wear a costume.*

ZOE. Hi Bill.

BILL *walks to a bowl of candy corn, picks one up, examines it, places it in his pocket, and exits.*

ZOE. Costume kicks ass, Bill.

P.A. *clicks on.*

P.A. SYSTEM. *[dogs barking]*
Ah, hello to the...teachers in the Faculty Room.

ZOE. Hello, Principal Dennis. It's just me here right now. Miss Bartholemhew.

P.A. SYSTEM. Well hello Miss Bartholemhew! And Happy Halloween!
How's the debate team doing? Are we going to get to the nationals?

ZOE. We...don't have a debate team, Principal Dennis – remember you decided to redirect the funds to Wrestling. Who, by the way, are doing great this season, so: kudos.

P.A. SYSTEM. Well, great, great.
How's the new P.A. System working out, in your opinion.

ZOE. Oh, it's–

P.A. SYSTEM. Now be honest Miss Bartholemhew!

ZOE. All right, it's–

P.A. SYSTEM. Because initially the overhaul *(extremely garbled; static) waah zxjfl arphs ldof...*

(His words continue at length, but indecipherable.)

(Finally, he stops talking.)

ZOE. Principal Dennis?

P.A. SYSTEM. Hmm?

ZOE. The new system's great.

P.A. SYSTEM. Fantastic!
And Mr. Durand. How does he seem to be working out so far?

ZOE. He's fine.

P.A. SYSTEM. Well that's a relief.

He had a rough time at his last school, but you teachers all bond, so I'm sure he's told you all about it…

[factory whistle]

Oooops!

…Sorry about that…still some bugs in the system!

And I spy with my little eye Mrs. Egan standing at the door of my office, which means I am about to be late to a meeting, so I'm going to sign off right now!

Glad we had this chat, Miss Bartholemhew.

[rooster crowing]

P.A. clicks off.

ADAM *and* **CARVER** *enter.* **ADAM** *carries a tambourine and* **CARVER** *carries a box of music.*

ADAM. It'll give it texture, it'll be uplifting!

CARVER. Just use it sparingly.

ADAM. *(to* **ZOE***)* When we sing the school anthem I'm going to play the tambourine.

CARVER. So long as it doesn't turn into a song *about* a tambourine.

ADAM. It won't. Hey, we just saw my girlfriend Jen Carlson in the parking lot and it looked like she was giving *Raphael* a ride somewhere.

ZOE. Feeling insecure?

ADAM. On the contrary. I was giving you a heads up in case you were worried about your guy…in case things weren't going A-OK. I mean, Jen dressed up as a nun this Halloween; that's not a coincidence. Anyway, while we're on the subject of, you know, boys and girls, we ran into Coach Salata in the halls and he brought you up again. Carver got *really* jealous.

CARVER. Fuck you.

ADAM. Coach Salata "likes" Zoe. You know once upon a time there were some football players – Coach Salata types – who wouldn't have fucked Zoe for *practice*. But *these* days, since his recent divorce from former cheerleader Kelli Keegan, Coach Salata "likes" Zoe, which is simply, simply, simply amazing.

ZOE. Lots of people like me, Adam.

ADAM. You know what, Sweetheart? I don't think that's true. Not even a little bit true. Nobody likes you. Coach Salata wants to fuck you, who can blame him, but he certainly doesn't like you. Principal Dennis doesn't like you – you freak him out. Every female teacher at Madison-Feurey loathes you. Come to think of it, I don't know anyone who likes you. Even you don't like you.

CARVER. I like her.

ADAM. No you don't, Carver, you just don't know what else to say. Come on, Zo, admit I'm right. You can't think of anyone who likes you. Anyone at all.

ZOE *is pale.*

Silence.

ADAM. I mean, really, who "likes" you.
Who likes you.

A beat.

ZOE. Raphael Gilberto likes me.

She exits.

ADAM *and* CARVER *sit in silence.*

ADAM. Well he has to like you because he's your boyfriend.

Blackout.

Scene Three

NOVEMBER

ZOE *and* **ADAM** *sit across from each other at the table.*
ZOE *staples cutout paper leaves to a long swath of fabric.*
When she finishes with one swath, she drapes it over a
chair.

We hear the KACHUNK of the stapler as **ZOE** *works.*

(KACHUNK)

(KACHUNK)

(KACHUNK)

ADAM *grades papers, scrawling loudly on each one*
and then turning it over. The KACHUNKS and the
SCRAWLS alternate.

ADAM. What are you doing.

(KACHUNK)

(KACHUNK)

ZOE. Crafts.

ADAM. Want to know what I'm doing.

ZOE. No.

ADAM. I'm grading Raphael Gilberto's paper.

(KACHUNK)

(KACHUNK)

ADAM. I'm giving him a "D." "Minus."

(KACHUNK)

ADAM. Kidding, Zoe, he's getting a very respectable B plus,
Zoe, you have to talk to me someday hello.

   CARVER *enters.*

ZOE. Hey, did you get my message last night?

CARVER. I did, I fell asleep in front of the TV, sorry.

ZOE. That's okay, did you bring the paint?

CARVER. Oh, damn, I left it on my desk, hold on. Hey, Adam.

ADAM. *(maniacally cheerful)* Good afternoon!

    CARVER *exits again.*

ADAM. Your good buddy Carver.

    (KACHUNK)

    (KACHUNK)

ADAM. Your dear, close pal Carver.

    I know what you're trying to do, and it's childish.

ZOE. Carver and I are friends, get over it.

ADAM. Has your chum Carver ever mentioned his old school?

ZOE. Don't get weird.

ADAM. I'll take that as a "no." No mention of the old school. That's interesting, you have to admit. I mean anytime we got a newbie before all we heard was, "We did it *this* way at my old school, la la la." Funny.

ZOE. I don't think it's a big deal.

ADAM. Well I do, I think it's a great big deal, and who doesn't love a mystery.

    (KACHUNK)

    ZOE *finishes and surveys her work.*

ZOE. That's going to have to do.

ADAM. What's a Fall Fling without fall foliage?

ZOE. Right.

ADAM. Polly Kamin told me what the thing is with exacto knives.

ZOE. Polly Kamin is doing a scene from ["Gossip Girl"]* for her semester project. I told everyone to choose a scene from contemporary drama. Polly taped an episode of ["Gossip Girl"], transcribed it, and that is her semester project. Which I have to grade.

---

* The name of the television show in brackets should be up-to-the-minute trendy, as well as appealing to fifteen-year-old girls. I prefer that it's not a rerun of an older show.

ADAM. Polly says that cutting is "in."

Little pause.

ADAM. Actually she showed me. One arm. Some of the girls are doing it. They trace long red lines on their arms and legs. Not deep. Not life-threatening. Just enough to break the skin. Just enough to leave an elegant scar. Exactos are better than razors, Polly said, because the handles afford better control. Isn't it great that they can get as many exactos as they need.

ZOE. Yeah, I believe Polly has a rosebud on her thigh. She's pretty good at it.

ADAM *watches her.*

ADAM. She's not an artist, though. Like Raphael. She's no "Still Waters Run Deep."

ZOE *meets his gaze.*

ZOE. Exact-o.

ADAM. Don't you want to be friends again.

ZOE. We're friends.

ADAM. ...Right, okay.

Hey! You should hear this. I got some papers back, and whose midterm turns out to be a fascinating read but Janet Lundquist! Subject? The prophet Zephaniah. Very big on heavy prophesies: "A day of wrath" blah blah blah.

Pause.

I'm going to read out loud in a moment, I'm just trying to find a sentence that has both a subject *and* a verb. Hold on...still looking...

Almost offhand.

Someday you're going to marry me again, Zoe, you'll marry me for real and that's going to be the Rapture.

ZOE *slaps* **ADAM** *full across the face.*

ADAM *slaps* **ZOE** *back, same strength.*

ZOE *slaps* **ADAM**.

ADAM *slaps* ZOE.

ZOE *slaps* ADAM.

ADAM *slaps* ZOE.

ZOE. Forget it!

You just asked me to marry you because I went to the Prom with Tony Wells.

ADAM. You know that is *bullshit!* Besides you said *yes.*

ZOE. And look what happened!

ADAM. Second marriages are always the happiest.

ZOE *slaps* ADAM.

ZOE. What is the matter with you? Have you been buying pot from Glenn Moller again?

ADAM. One time, one time, and you smoked it with me!

ZOE. I didn't know you bought it from *Glenn!*

ADAM. You're hardly in a position to be judgmental.

ZOE. Yes I am! Glenn's weed is terrible. He ripped you off.

ADAM. What's the alternative!

ZOE. What do you mean.

ADAM. Who else deals.

ZOE. I'm not telling! I thought that was a onetime transgression, Adam, I was willing to let it lie, but if you're going to become a guy who scores pot off Glenn, I mean please, that's unbearably boring.

ADAM. Ahhh! There it is: "boring." My behavior is "boring."

ZOE. Don't start–

ADAM. Make no mistake, I admire it, I mean Zoe when you say something is boring, it's not just *dull;* I might as well crumple it up and throw it away. I might as well set it on fire. When you say something is boring, it becomes utterly worthless, the *idea* is worthless, *talking* about it is worthless, and that I even *entertained* such an idea for a minute makes *me* worthless...and I want to be worth something because I want to go to the Rapture.

ZOE. You want to go to the Rapture.

ADAM. Maybe. Maybe I do.

According to "Sudden Awakening," *Volume Three,* all it takes is one good thing, one action that you do with a pure heart – and you get to go. Whssh.

ZOE. Are you drunk?

ADAM. "Are you buying pot?" "Are you drunk?" What's with you and the–

Yeah, I am a little drunk. Why do you ask.

Little pause.

ZOE. No reason.

ADAM. You don't care.

ZOE. No, I don't.

ADAM. I hate Thanksgiving. I hate this month, it's so desolate, flat, brown. When I get up in the morning I look in the refrigerator and I stare at the corn bran, and then I stare at the milk, and then I stare at the orange juice and vodka and I pick.

ZOE. I guess you do.

ADAM. Don't act like we're so different, cause we're exactly the same.

ZOE. If it comforts you to imagine that, by all means go ahead.

ADAM. Zing! Good one! Dismissive, contemptuous, and pithy!

Little pause.

ZOE. Raphael told me –

ADAM. *(instant interruption)*

Don't ever talk about me with Raphael.

P.A. SYSTEM *clicks on.*

P.A. SYSTEM. *[big Charlie Chan Gong]*

P.A. SYSTEM *clicks off.*

ZOE. Well, time for class. Raphael's directing his scene today. He picked one from Ibsen.

ZOE *mimes shooting herself in the mouth and exits. We can hear* **CARVER** *in the hallway outside.*

CARVER. *(unseen)* Darby, if you want to discuss *other* ways to earn extra credit, see me after class.

CARVER *enters.*

CARVER. *(a sigh)* How's it going.

ADAM. *(reading)* Listen to my girlfriend's essay. OK. "In a post-apocalyptic world, what can one expect" – *one,* that's so cute – "of those who are left behind, *suddenly awake* to the real reality of the rapture?" – Real reality. Did I mention that my kids have put together a "Sudden Awakening" Book Club?

CARVER. No kidding.

ADAM. I'm very proud. I'm the faculty advisor.

CARVER. Do you have Darby Weider in any of your classes?

ADAM. Oh, sure. She's a kook. Got her paper in here some-where.

CARVER. She's barefoot today. She's always barefoot.

ADAM. Well she's a hippie.

CARVER. But it's thirty degrees outside! She could get frost-bite! That's not being a hippie, it's being stupid!

ADAM. She's a stupid hippie.

CARVER. She's not stupid, she's a straight-A student.
I don't think she wears underwear.

ADAM. Well, that's ironic.
I mean, it's wasted on you. Although, come to think of it, Darby *is* sort of androgynous…with some imagina-tion…

CARVER. That's not funny.

ADAM. *(a concession)* Maybe it's not.

CARVER. She just stopped me in the hall. She's barefoot, she's hacked off all her hair, and she's wearing this awful tight white sweater dress that barely covers her… anything.

CARVER *shakes his head, pained.*

CARVER. Darby wanted to tell me that she was from "somewhere else." "I'm not from here." I said, what does that mean? She said, "That's why I cut my hair." She said I was a sign.

ADAM. *You're* a sign? Was she talking about the last chapter of Book Two?

CARVER. I don't know. She went into some detail that was very hard to follow. She also asked for course credit if she performed "a ritual under an open sky" – which, obviously, is not going to happen.

ADAM. Did she say *spring* ritual? "Winter is a time of spiritual solstice, but with Spring comes ritual?"

CARVER. *(exasperated)* I don't know!

   ADAM *considers.*

ADAM. How many advisees do you have?

CARVER. Thirty-nine.

ADAM. That's a lot.

CARVER. I know.

ADAM. Hell, one more's not going to make a difference to me, toss Darby my way.

CARVER. That's not – really?

ADAM. Sure.

CARVER. You could do that?

ADAM. You have a lot on your plate, right? You're doing Spirit Days. I know Darby from last year, she's a bookworm, it's no big deal.

CARVER. And you'll look out for any signs…

ADAM. My specialty.

CARVER. That, that would be great. She's… Honestly, I just don't want to do the wrong thing.

ADAM. File the papers with Melanie in the front office.

CARVER. Great. Great.

   ADAM *reads. He lights a marijuana pipe, tokes.*

CARVER. Oh, Jesus!

ADAM. *(reading)* Yeah, he's the Man.

CARVER. Adam!

No response.

CARVER. Has it occurred to you that maybe you should try to curtail the drug use?

ADAM. No. God these kids are hacks.

CARVER. Why don't you teach them *not* to be?!

ADAM. Yeah, there it is…that tone. The dulcet tones that go bong bong bong – I'm judging you!

> **CARVER***: deep breath. Steels himself to tell the Truth in a tough-love kind of way.*

CARVER. Adam, I appreciate your taking on Darby Weider. But I don't buy the Big-Man-On-Campus act. Why don't you put this infantile bullshit behind you? I mean, *I'm* trying, *Zoe's* trying. What are *you* doing?

> **ADAM** *closes a paper he's reading, narrows his eyes.*

ADAM. *Zoe's* trying.

CARVER. Yes, she is. We both are.

ADAM. Zoe and you. Remaking the system.

CARVER. Go ahead, say something snide.

ADAM. No, no; nothing snide to say.

CARVER. Yeah, right.

ADAM. I'm just – whoo. You took my breath away there for a sec. Zoe and you. Fighting the good fight. Isn't life a funny old thing.

I met someone who *knows* you.

You don't look surprised. Aren't you surprised? I mean, you're a long way from home. Let me tell you how it happened: I went to the SuperMart across the river and in the bargain liquor section I got into a friendly argument with this lady about the best way to make a vodka stinger (results TBA). Anyway she happened to be a *teacher!* And in fact she used to be a colleague of *yours!*

Pause.

ADAM. And you know it was funny, I had no idea *where* you taught. In the city. I don't believe you ever mentioned that. And this woman, oh shit, what was her name, Mickey. No, Nicky. Micky. Volare, Volak–

CARVER. Nicky Volansky.

ADAM. *Yes!* She used to teach in the city, so she told me and something clicked in the back of my mind and I went, hey, did you know a Carver Durand and she did!

CARVER. Huh.

ADAM. So I guess that means you knew her, right?

CARVER. Not well.

ADAM. Well that is fascinating, Carver, you're a fascinating guy. She was pretty closemouthed about you. It was almost weird. All she said was that you had missed her retirement party. And that they had all enjoyed working with you at Lincoln. And she was Very Sorry that you had left so *abruptly.*

Lincoln High. This was the school where there was some kind of, what was it, *arson?*

CARVER. You must be thinking about some other place.

ADAM. Must be.

She gave me her number. Becky.

CARVER. Nicky.

ADAM. Bicky. Invited me over for Thanksgiving dinner, actually, but I had to say no, cause I have other plans.

CARVER. And what are those.

ADAM. Well I'm going to my girlfriend's house. Duh. Jen Carlson's mother is going to roast the shit out of something that her father shot, and we're all going to eat it, and I'll talk about what a good student Jen is, and I imagine we'll close out the evening with some pie and chat about the Rapture. Jen has developed a real interest in the "Sudden Awakening" series. I smell a new Book Club recruit!

I imagine Zoe is spending Thanksgiving with her boyfriend.

CARVER. I wouldn't know.

ADAM. When I think about all my Thanksgivings with Zoe, Carver? It's like remembering heaven. Our first Thanksgiving, we went to Denny's, had the grand slam breakfast for dinner. Bliss. So Carv, you want to tell me your Thanksgiving plans? Huh?

CARVER. Why waste the breath?

ADAM. *(jovial)* Why indeed, why indeed. That's a little piece of Euclidian logic, there, pal.

ADAM reads, flipping through the papers.

Oh look, here's an essay from Darby, *my brand new advisee.*

He reads.

CARVER. Well?

ADAM keeps reading.

CARVER. What'd she write?

ADAM. Darby wrote about Icarus.

ADAM hands **CARVER** *the paper;* **CARVER** *reads. After a moment:*

CARVER. "Icarus was the son of an overbearing father, a man who could not bear for his child to be free. But Icarus understood what freedom was worth. Icarus placed the wings that his father had crafted on his shoulders, and he soared up towards the sun. He released himself from the boundaries of this world: he flew."

CARVER *is moved by the essay.*

ADAM *stares at* **CARVER** *intently.*

ADAM. What the hell are you doing here, Carver.

The closet door opens, sort of suddenly. **BILL** *steps out.* **CARVER** *is quite startled.* **BILL**'s *expression, as always, is blank. He sniffs deeply. He stands in the center of the room for a moment. Takes a comb out of his pocket. Combs his hair for a longer-than-normal period of time.* **CARVER** *and* **ADAM** *watch.* **BILL** *puts his comb away and exits.*

CARVER. Do you think…was he…

ADAM. Yes.

CARVER. Do you know what I was going to ask?

ADAM. Who cares.

CARVER. ...What's in there?

ADAM. Narnia.

>   **CARVER** *opens the door and peers into the dark closet.*
>   *He pokes around the coats. Goes in farther.* **ADAM** *walks*
>   *behind him, shuts the door, and locks it with a distinc-*
>   *tive CLICK.*

CARVER. *(muffled)* Hey! Hey!

>   Okay, ha ha ha.

>   *Unhurriedly,* **ADAM** *takes out a flask, sips, puts some*
>   *stray papers in order, and departs.*

CARVER. You got me: very funny!

>   Adam.

>   Adam.

>   Okay, enough's enough.

>   ADAM. HEY.

>   Let me out.

>   LET ME OUT, YOU ASSHOLE!

>   **P.A. SYSTEM** *clicks on.*

P.A. SYSTEM. *[cow lowing]*

>   Good afternoon, and time for our after-lunch an-
>   nouncements. * Remember that during this Season of
>   Thanks, we're collecting food for those less fortunate...

* **CARVER.** *(overlap; muffled yelling over the P.A.)*

>   HEY! HEY! SOMEONE COME IN HERE AND LET
>   ME OUT!

>   Helllooo.

>   Let me out!

P.A. SYSTEM. I'll just wait until everyone is listening attentively.

CARVER. I'm in the closet! Hello! I'm in the closet!

P.A. SYSTEM. I'm still waiting.

>   *Blackout.*

Scene Four

DECEMBER

Something about the lights tells us it's nighttime.

Techno dance music can be heard faintly, coming from the gym — music from the Winter Semiformal.

ADAM *sits behind the couch. He wears a suit. He has a sock puppet with big googly eyes on each hand. Or maybe the puppets are realistic, like the ones that Mr. Rogers used.* **ADAM** *uses the back of the couch as a stage.*

SOCK PUPPET #1. "I'm Holden Caulfield and I'm a disenchanted teenager!"

ADAM. Aw. Holden, what's the matter?

HOLDEN PUPPET. "I just got kicked out of school! But I don't care, cause everyone's a phony."

ADAM. Huh. Everyone?

HOLDEN PUPPET. "Yeah! Everyone! Except maybe this one girl…but she's probably a phony, too."

ADAM. She probably is.

HOLDEN PUPPET. "Why can't people just love each other?"

ADAM. You're kind of a whiny guy, aren't you Holden.

HOLDEN PUPPET. "Go to hell! You're a phony, too!"

ADAM. Maybe so. Maybe so. But who's *this?*

His other hand joins them. A new puppet.

SOCK PUPPET #2. "I'm J.D. Salinger."

ADAM. The recluse!

J.D. SALINGER PUPPET. "Yes, and I created the character of Holden Caulfield, and I haven't granted you permission to portray that character."

ADAM. Oh yeah? What are you going to do about it?

J.D. SALINGER PUPPET. "This recluse is gonna kick your ass!"

J.D. *picks up a [real] gun, which* **J.D.** *points at* **ADAM** *and pretend-fires.*

J.D. SALINGER PUPPET. "*BLAM!*"

ADAM. Ahhh!

He falls with a thud behind the couch, unseen. The puppets look down at him.

HOLDEN PUPPET. "That guy was an asshole."

The puppets disappear as **ADAM***'s arms drop limply to his sides. He's hidden.*

Sound of running in the hall. The door bangs open and **CARVER** *and* **ZOE** *fall into the room, all giggles, like kids.*

ZOE *wears a beautiful closefitting shiny dress, and has long gloves that go to mid-bicep, like a princess.*

CARVER *wears a sharp dark suit and tie.*

When the door is opened, the techno music gets momentarily louder.

P.A. SYSTEM *clicks on.*

P.A. SYSTEM. *[harpsichord rendering of musical phrase "and a partridge in a pear tree"]*
Good evening, students and teachers, Principal Dennis here to welcome you to the annual Madison-Feurey Christmas Formal. Let's take a moment to identify an Important Rule for tonight's Dance.
The rule is simple: "Be Good." Not hard to remember. Be good. Avoid inappropriate behavior. *(musing)* What does "inappropriate" mean? It means "*not* appropriate." Which means "not right; not right now." In short, just do your best.
This is Principal Dennis saying Ho Ho Ho.

[reindeer bells jingling]

P.A. SYSTEM *clicks off.*

ZOE. I want to find Bill. I need to dance with Bill.

CARVER *opens the closet door.*

ZOE. What are you doing?
CARVER. Nothing.

ZOE. Ooh, I almost forgot, you need a boutonnière. I made you a craft boutonnière! Here...

From her purse, she extracts a big pink paper flower and pins it on **CARVER**'s *lapel.*

ZOE. I made it pink.

CARVER. Very thoughtful.

Music changes. It's something like, "Sleepwalk." He and **ZOE** *slow dance.*

CARVER. Bring a date?

ZOE. No, I'm stag.

CARVER. *(lame attempt at joking)* Except for your boyfriend.

ZOE. Well of course. I'd never hurt Raphael's feelings like that.

Still dancing...

CARVER. *(uncomfortable)* Right. Raphael. Ha.
Tell me about your Winter Semiformal. Back in the day.

ZOE. I had a dark green taffeta dress. Adam wore a bow tie the exact same shade of green. But he wasn't my date. Mr. Younger and I have been around a long time.

CARVER. And neither of you ever left.

ZOE. Nope.

CARVER. Why'd you get married; why'd you get divorced; were you ever in love...

ZOE. Why does anybody do anything? Because you want the rush, you want something *more* than just your, your own mundane self, you want to be *awake.*

A little moment.

ZOE. And then you realize that a young marriage maybe isn't that.
I went away to college for a year. Not far, just over in Little Eden. But, "away." So...we were apart for that time. The whole time, I kept waiting for someone else to, to look at me the way that Adam looked at me. And nobody did. So I came home.
You think Adam's a bad influence on me.

CARVER. I think he's a bad influence on everybody.

ZOE. Adam's not *strong* enough to be really *bad*.

CARVER. Come on.

ZOE. He's a good teacher.

CARVER. We should be doing things that matter.

ZOE. Are we doing things that matter?

CARVER. I think so.

ZOE. Let's stop talking about Adam. Let's talk about you.
Tell me something delicious about your past.

CARVER. I'm very dull.
I teach. That's it.

ZOE. Do you have family in the city?

CARVER. My parents are dead.

ZOE. Huh. Brothers or sisters?

CARVER. No.

ZOE. No one to track you down to find out who you really
are, hm.

ADAM. *(popping into sight)* And don't you find that astonish-
ingly coincidental?

ZOE. God! What are you doing there?!

ADAM. I'm sorry. Did I interrupt something?

ZOE. Don't be stupid. Are you spying on me?

ADAM. Not spying at all, sweetheart, *stalking*. And thank you
for saying I was a good teacher – that warms my heart.
You wanted to know something about Carver, right? As
it turns out I know someone who knows Carver – *you*
remember, Carver, Nicky Volansky? – well she and I
spent some quality time together recently and I found
out a tidbit or two.

CARVER. Come on Zoe, we should get back and help serve
the punch.

ADAM. No no no don't go! Not before I tell you about the
little assignation, a li'l dark secret from Carver's past.

As a puppet.

ADAM. "Zoe, you look beautiful!"

In his regular voice.

Big News: Our Buddy Carver was *fired from his last job because he had an affair with a student!*

Silence.

CARVER. That's not true.

ADAM. I should clarify: I don't know for certain whether they pink-slipped you because you had an *affair* or whether it was because your student *set himself on fire*.

I saw newspaper clippings! That Nicky Vollansky, she's a clipper. A sixteen year-old genius named Sam. He wrote love letters to you...lots of letters...pages and pages of letters...

CARVER. You don't have any fucking clue what you're talking about.

ADAM. ...And then Sam set himself on fire because you broke it off! I knew I remembered hearing *something* about Lincoln...but it wasn't *arson.* Your student *immolated* himself. For love! Should have been a national story – can you imagine the coverage – but his parents had money. That's what Nicky Volansky said. She's a very informed clipper, Nicky Volansky.

You walk around here and you act so smug. Mr. Good Intentions! You plan Spirit Days, and you write anthems, and you act weepy about poor barefoot Darby boo hoo who incidentally is doing fine, and in the meantime your ex-boyfriend from Lincoln High is a charcoal briquette.

CARVER. Don't listen to him. *(to ADAM)* You're an asshole.

ADAM. Yeah, and who are you? You're a History teacher who *set a kid on fire!*

CARVER. *I never touched him!* He did it *himself* on the quad –

A moment.

CARVER. He...

It was after school.

I wasn't there.

CARVER. He soaked his clothes in gasoline, and his hair. And lit a match.

And…

ADAM. Pffft.

They released only one letter–

CARVER. It wasn't a letter, it was an essay. About wanting to be a Phoenix. Rising from ashes.

ADAM. You've been holding out. And we tell you just about everything.

ZOE. You feeling pretty good, Adam?

ADAM. I feel A-OK, yeah.

ZOE. This is a pathetic display.

ADAM. Yeah, you must be bored. That was some *boring* news. You know babe, Raphael got to the dance early. And damn if it didn't *look like* he was *waiting* for someone.

ZOE. Well he wasn't.

ADAM. I say he was. Anyway, just before I came in here, I saw your boyfriend in a *heavy* making out session with one of the Severine Twins. Wish I could say which, but I've never been able to tell them apart. Always give 'em both a B plus.

Zo? You hear me?

ZOE. I heard you.

ADAM. So what are you going to do? A Severine twin is getting biblical with Raphael! You gonna kick her ass, or do you feel you have an unfair advantage because of the age thing.

ZOE. Fuck off.

ADAM. Unlike your fickle Raphael, my girlfriend Jen Carlson falls more in love with me by the day. She's wearing a dress that's the same color as my cummerbund.

CARVER. Adam, everyone knows that Jen is in love with Raphael.

ADAM. *(jovially)* Stay out of it, firestarter.

Raphael's got his hand on the tit of Severine number one. Jen'll get over it. But it looks like the beginning of a whole new world for Still Waters Run Deep. No kidding. You better check it out.

ZOE *starts to exit, fast.*

CARVER. Zoe, wait –

ZOE *looks at* CARVER. *Then she's out the door.*

ADAM. It's My Party And I'll Cry If I Want To…You really think I have a decent voice? Can I still play the tambourine for Spirit Days?

CARVER. Fuck you.

ADAM. You're not the sign, pal. I don't care what Darby says.

CARVER. I don't know what you think you're doing, or what you want.

ADAM. Sure you do. You were dancing with it. I want the Rapture.

Zoe doesn't get what you're up to. But I get it. You blow up your boyfriend, take off, try to make a break with the past. Shed your skin. Be somebody new. Maybe even get married, have a wife, a dog, an unsullied history. And who better to partner you on your new path than my Zo.

You want the Rapture, too.

CARVER. I want to *teach.* I want a calm, effective learning environment. I want to help students improve. I want to be good at –

ADAM. *(interrupting)* Whssh!

CARVER. You want the Rapture? You're not going to get it.

ADAM. Ooh, that looks like a gauntlet on the floor.

CARVER *slams out the door.*

ADAM. *(to sock puppet)* Well, back to the dance.

(as sock puppet) "Right on."

(as himself) Right on.

The puppet disposes of ADAM*'s gun in the gun chute.* ADAM *turns out the lights in the faculty room and exits. Eerie florescent light shines through the mottled glass panel on the door.*

Sound of footsteps running down the hall.

ZOE *re-enters the faculty room, but she does not turn on the lights.*

She walks around the room unsteadily, shell-shocked, her arms wrapped around herself, becoming increasingly agitated.

Quite suddenly, she bursts into tears: heaving, ugly sobs that wrack her like cramps. She doubles over, keening. Her crying is a tidal wave, her face a grimace. She tears at her corsage and throws it across the room, she stumbles and crumples onto the couch, curling into a fetal position, weeping.

ZOE. Aahhhhh–

ZOE *jumps up, opens a drawer so that the contents spill noisily onto the floor. She finds what she wants, slim and silver. It's an exacto knife.*

She takes off one of her long gloves and gently, deliberately draws the exacto knife up one bare arm.

A single long line of blood appears.

ZOE *sighs a deep breath of relief.*

She has stopped weeping. She takes off her other glove.

Her face is tranquil, composed, at peace.

Blackout.

Scene Five

JANUARY

The faculty room is empty.

P.A. SYSTEM. *[egg timer ticking for an inordinately long time to alarm brrrring]*
Good morning Madison-Feurey High, Principal Dennis here wishing you a Happy. New. Year. I know we're all raring to go after a restful winter break. And this week our very own Cardinals take flight on the court – the first game of the semester, against the Chesterfield Shredders, is Thursday Night! Let's see you all there! Principal Dennis saying, that's all for now.

[sound of applause, cheering]

You're too kind.

[dog barking]

P.A. SYSTEM *clicks off.)*ADAM *enters, humming. He tapes up a Book Club flyer.*

CARVER *enters, bundled up and brushing snow off himself.*

ADAM. How was your Christmas vacation, buddy?

CARVER. That's none of your business.

ADAM. I prefer "beeswax." Seen Zoe yet?

CARVER. No.

ADAM. Really. Well she looks great. *(re: flyer)*
Want to come to Book Club after school?

CARVER. Thanks but I'll pass.

ADAM. You're missing out. Darby's president. She's really rallying the other kids. We're up to "Sudden Awakening," Volume Five. It's got it all: history, prophecy, and the Horsemen of the Apocalypse.

ZOE *enters. She looks different. She wears baggy clothes, several long sleeved t-shirts layered over one another, jeans that are too big. The effect should be both hip – she* *should look much younger – and strange, as though at first glance she could be a street kid.*

Another thing: she also looks radiantly happy.

ADAM. *(to* **ZOE***)* I know what's going on. You hear me? I know what's going on.

ZOE. I'm sure.

ADAM. I'm *very clear* about what's going on. Very clear. You make my head hurt. My head hurts. Oh, damn damn damn.

ZOE. Get an aspirin from the nurse.

ADAM. I'm going to. *(pointing)* I'm not done talking to you. Either of you.

ADAM *exits.*

Awkward silence.

CARVER. *(re: her clothes)* Wassup Gee.

No response.

CARVER. That was a joke.

ZOE. "Ha."

CARVER. Ha.

Anyway. Called you over vacation.

ZOE. I was pretty busy.

CARVER. How was your break?

ZOE. Fine.

She busies herself with papers.

CARVER. We should talk.

ZOE. If you want.

CARVER. I want to explain about some of the things that Adam said the night of the Christmas dance…I don't want you to have the wrong idea –

ZOE. *(interrupting)* The "wrong idea!" You – you know *rolled your eyes* every time I talked about *my* boyfriend!

CARVER. That's your thing with Adam! I don't want to get into that!

ZOE. "Get into that!" You're in! You and your old boyfriend from "out of town."

CARVER. He wasn't my boyfriend! Sam was my student. My student.

ZOE. You have the nerve to talk about "doing things that matter." Were *all* his teachers fired?

CARVER. He saw me as a, a mentor. When he…hurt himself, and the school found out *I* was gay, and I was his favorite teacher, that was it.

ZOE. Right.

CARVER. That's what happened.

ZOE. How about the letters?

There were letters, right? Lots?

Little pause.

CARVER. Just because he wrote me letters and I'm not saying he did, doesn't mean that he was, that we were together.

ZOE. *(losing interest)* Well if that's what you say happened then that's what happened.

ZOE *opens a note folded origami-style, reads it, giggles.*

CARVER. *(trying to regain normalcy)* What are you reading?

ZOE. It's personal.

CARVER. So…are we okay.

ZOE. Let's just move into the new semester, shall we.

ZOE *puts headphones on and listens. She's really into the music, which we can't hear. She takes out a Twinkie and plastic knife, cuts the top of the Twinkie off lengthwise, sprinkles some Fritos atop the cream, replaces the top, bites. She eats, drinks a Coke, ignores* CARVER.

ADAM *enters again.*

ADAM. That doesn't look very healthy. Right, Carver?

CARVER. Not my business.

ADAM. Good boundary setting, pal. *(loud)* ZOE, ENJOYING YOUR MUSIC?

ZOE. YEAH.

ADAM. HOW'D YOU KNOW ABOUT *[names the group she's listening to]***?

ZOE. I SAW A VIDEO.

ADAM. YOU DON'T HAVE A TV.

> **ZOE** *takes off the headphones.*

ZOE. Yes I do.

ADAM. No you don't. You've never had a TV, you hate TV.

ZOE. Well I don't anymore.

ADAM. Carver, you know Zoe doesn't have a TV, right? You're her buddy, you know that: no TV. *(to* **ZOE***)* What are you eating?

ZOE. A snack.

ADAM. You're a *vegan*.

ZOE. People change.

ADAM. No more carrot sticks? No more celery strips? No cliff bars or raisins or apples.

> **ADAM** *goes through* **ZOE***'s bag. He pulls out Twinkies, Dingdongs, bags of chips, a coke – lots of junk food.*

ZOE. If you find anything you want, help yourself.

> **ADAM** *becomes increasingly manic and upset by the food in her bag.*

ADAM. All right. I get it. You want to play that way, fine. I'm taking this!

> *He slams out with a Ding Dong.*

> **ZOE** *puts her music back on.* **CARVER** *turns it off.*

CARVER. Don't you think we should do something?

ZOE. About what? Adam? Who else would do English Comp? They'd never find anyone to come here midterm. He can actually be a pretty incredible English teacher. He has this assignment where each student

---

** The band should be real, currently popular, and preferably indie rather than mainstream.

chooses a character from a Salinger story and a character from Greek mythology and then we'd write a conversation between the two... well anyway there's nobody in the district who'd take over a spot now so the point's moot.

Next week I have to have auditions for the spring play and I haven't decided what the play's going to be. Although *Darby* had a suggestion for me. Your hippie.

CARVER. She's Adam's advisee now.

ZOE. Since when?

CARVER. Before Christmas.

ZOE. Well, that explains a lot. She handed me a proposal for a "play" which she called a "free adaptation" from one of those "Suddenly Awake" novels. Her writing skills aren't bad but the source material – pee-yew.

CARVER. Is it, does it have something to do with a ritual? She's obsessed with this spring ritual.

ZOE. She's obsessed with you.

CARVER. I am not the problem! If anything, those *books–*

ZOE. *(interrupting)* Oh, she's one of the Rapture kids, big deal. And you know she used to be a real loner but she has quite a group gathered around her these days, so consider that a good sign.

> **BILL** *enters with briefcase and goes to get a cup of coffee. When he turns his back to us, we see that he has a handwritten sign taped to his back. It reads "WAKE UP."* **ZOE** *takes it off him as he begins to exit.*

ZOE. Bill.

> *She hands it to him. He reads it, places it in his briefcase, exits.*

CARVER. Listen, Zoe, have you seen my sheet music around here? I wanted to make up a little booklet for Spirit Days.
...Zoe?

ZOE. Have you ever noticed Raphael's smell?

CARVER. His…smell.

ZOE. Raphael smells like fresh baked bread. His skin smells like a scone. His hair smells like cinnamon. You cannot believe how good he smells. It's like smelling creation. It's Biblical. He smells like the beginning of the world. *(She sniffs, holds out her arm, smiling.)* Here – it's on my wrist.

Little silence.

CARVER. I should get to class.

ZOE. Raphael beat me at PlayStation yesterday, but I'm getting better. I'm starting to give him a really good game. We play "Bomb Squad" to see who can defuse the bomb the fastest. I'm getting better every time.

Scene Six

FEBRUARY

CARVER *leans out the doorway, lecturing several students, his back to the faculty room.* **ADAM** *reclines on the couch, reading.*

CARVER. *(raised voice)* I don't care who started what, *you* are not entitled to the entire hall, and *you* can't curse at them if they happen to be in your path. Do I make myself clear?

Mumbled assent – should be unintelligible.

CARVER. *(raised voice)* All right, it's over. Get to class.

He shuts the door.

CARVER. Why is your Book Club out looking for a *rumble?*

ADAM. A "rumble?" Are we in *West Side Story?*

CARVER. You know what I mean. They move through the halls together in a, a clump.

ADAM. Book Club's an intense group of literate teens.

CARVER. They're *alienating.*

ADAM. You wouldn't be alienated if you read the books.

CARVER *unpacks his lunch.*

We can hear faint singing from outside.

CARVER. *(listening)* Is someone singing…the anthem?

They are.

ADAM. I think they're working on something for Spirit days.

CARVER *looks pleased.*

A commotion in the hall outside.

ZOE. *(loud; unseen; outside the door)* I'm *not* making it a big deal! You said you'd call last night, and then you didn't.

Again, it's important that Raphael's lines are unintelligible – we hear a young voice, mumbling.

ZOE. Oh, please.

Raphael – something unintelligible.

ZOE. What*ever!*

> ZOE *enters, slamming door, wiping her eyes. She wears jeans and many, many t-shirts, even more layers than the last scene. Her hair is in a baseball cap, maybe.*
>
> ADAM *stares at her coldly and exits.*
>
> *She sits and takes out her lunch, a pack of sno-balls.*

CARVER. You missed Parent-Teacher Conferences last night.

> ZOE *wipes her eyes, stuffs most of a sno-ball in her mouth.*

ZOE. *(mouth full)* Sorry.

Can I have some of your milk?

> *She drinks.*

CARVER. At my old school they stopped having conferences because nobody came. But last night was solid.

ZOE. Uh huh.

CARVER. I was in charge of the Spirit Days Booth, I talked to a lot of parents and the feedback overall was really positive. Spirit Days are totally coming together. Monday, the freshmen are resurrecting the traditional bake sale. Tuesday, the sophmores put on a pageant of the masters. Wednesday is junior trivia bowl, Thursday's All-School Color Wars, and then on the Last Day we have the rally. Where were you?

ZOE. Making Valentines.

> *She takes out some construction paper and proceeds to industriously cut out hearts, gluing them to doilies, etc., for the remainder of the scene.* CARVER *watches.*

CARVER. ...Right.

Loren Elliot is dealing E.

ZOE. I thought it was acid.

CARVER. It's E.

ZOE. Wow.

CARVER. I just sent Naomi Sanger home. This morning in class, I asked her about President Grover Cleveland and she said that he was "a beautiful, beautiful man, who had some fucking rad policies."

ZOE. She got it from Loren? He is such a supernerd.

CARVER. With E. Don't tell Adam.

ZOE. Have you noticed that Jen Carlson has buddied up with Darby? That is such a total crop circle. They're as thick as thieves. Things change.

CARVER. It's fortuitous that you mention Jen Carlson, because I wanted to ask you if you've noticed anything unusual about her lately.

Silence.

CARVER. Like for example have you noticed that she weighs, I'm guessing, 90 pounds.

ZOE. Polly said that she took Jen to Psych Services.

CARVER. Once.

ZOE. So: progress.

CARVER. When she turns sideways she almost flickers out. She's still very fragile over…
She's starving herself.

ZOE. No joke, I should fail her for her breath alone.

CARVER. You're *failing* her?!

ZOE. She's getting an F on her midterm acting project.

CARVER. Don't do that. You can't do that.

ZOE. Excuse me. She's constantly late, and for her midterm she read this half-assed monologue written by none other than Darby.

CARVER. What monologue.

ZOE. Oh you know, thunder, lightning, people growing wings, flights of angels, a hodgepodge of Greek mythology and the Bible and who knows what else. *Dawson's Creek.* "Then there shall be *fire*, then there shall be *rain*" – it's like the Book of Revelations as told to James Taylor.

CARVER. You can't just *fail* her, she's under a lot of stress.

ZOE. Hello! Jen is not doing the work.

CARVER. *She has a broken heart!*

ZOE. Hey, that's what happens! You're sixteen, and your heart breaks, and then you're twenty-two, and your heart breaks, and then you're thirty, and guess what– your heart breaks again! In the meantime you wipe your eyes and show up for your midterms!

CARVER. That is…really mean.

   ZOE ignores him.

CARVER. Why didn't you come to Parent-Teacher Conferences?

ZOE. I was *busy*, I told you.

CARVER. Busy. Making Valentines – for who?

ZOE. FOR THE CLASS.

CARVER. Bullshit. *Look* at you! Look at yourself!

   ZOE lazily gives him the finger.

CARVER. You are ignoring students in *trouble*. You are fighting with students in the *hallway*.

ZOE. It was just a tiff!

CARVER. I've heard the rumors. Everyone has. Raphael might take Andra Tilson to the Prom!

ZOE. *(sharp)* Andra Tilson is a *cow*. What's the matter, Carver, you jealous?! Why don't you take another look at Darby? I wonder if she doesn't feel *abandoned*.

CARVER. *(inarticulately furious)* Fuck you! Fuck you! Fuck you fuck you fuck you.

   ADAM *enters.*

ADAM. I'm back.

CARVER. Fuck you!

   He slams out.

   ZOE calmly returns to her Valentine-making.

ADAM. What's with him.

ZOE. Bent out of shape about the parent-teacher conferences.

ADAM. Well we all missed you last night.

ZOE. You were there. Color me surprised.

ADAM. I used to go all the time. Back in the day. Where I met *your* parents.

ZOE. *(changing subject)* Carver told me that Loren Elliot's dealing E.

ADAM. No kidding. Loren Elliot.

Offering his own news.

Darby has been writing scene after scene of this Rapture play.

ZOE. Is that what it is. Jen performed some of it.

ADAM. Carver is a character, did you know that?

ZOE. What does that mean he's a character.

ADAM. He's a character in Darby's play. The character's not *named* Carver but it most definitely is him.

ZOE. How do you know?

ADAM. I teach English Zoe, I can spot thinly veiled characters, it's in my job description.

ZOE. What is Darby doing writing a play about Carver?

ADAM. Please, don't overstate; it's not "about" Carver per se.

ZOE. Well what *is* it about.

Little beat.

ADAM. It's a work in progress.

ZOE. Has Carver read it?

ADAM. No.

ZOE. *Should* he?

ADAM. He'll get to *see* it soon enough.

ZOE. What happens to his character?

ADAM. What do you think happens. He wakes up. Suddenly.

ZOE. Is this Rapture play a comedy? Or a tragedy?

ADAM. It's everything, babe.

Making some Valentines there I see.

That's one of the first memories I have about you. Have I ever told you that?

ZOE. *(deep craft concentration on her doily)* Every Valentine's Day.

ADAM. I remember looking at you during study hall, and I walked over to you and I whispered, "What are you doing?" and you said, "Everyone deserves a Valentine."

ZOE. And you said, "Even Fred?"

ADAM. Fred Linter.

ZOE. Remember him?

ADAM. Please, who could forget. Poor guy was balding at seventeen. He looked like a monk with zits.

> **ZOE** *starts laughing really, really hard. So does* **ADAM** – *a shared memory.*

ADAM. He smelled, I don't know, like *baloney* all the time… which was bizarre since didn't he claim to be a vegetarian?…

> **ZOE** *laughs more.*

ADAM. And everyone in class started calling him "Brother Linter."

ZOE. I know…OW!

> **ZOE** *has cut her thumb with an exacto knife while making a heart. She laughs harder, then weirdly, instantaneously, begins to cry.*

ADAM. Hey. Hey. You're okay. It's okay.

> **ZOE** *cries so hard it's difficult to understand her speech.* **ADAM** *comforts her.*

ZOE. I know

I just

ADAM. Shh. Valentines are a heavy responsibility.

> *She laughs a little but still cries.* **ADAM** *strokes her hair. He is very gentle.*

ZOE. I'm just
I feel so tired

ADAM. Shh.
I know.
Hey. Hey Zoe.

ZOE. Hey.

ADAM. It's me. You know me.

ZOE. I know.

Little silence. They are close together.

ADAM. Where've you been, huh?

ZOE. What do you mean.

ADAM. You've been gone a while, I've missed my Zoe, where are you…

ZOE. Not "your" Zoe.

ADAM. I need to ask you something serious.

ZOE. Don't.

ADAM. I have to.

ZOE. No you don't.

ADAM. Yes I do. For real.
Zoe. We didn't do this right before. I just want to…do one good thing.

ZOE. *(overlapping)* What does that mean?

ADAM. It means I want to do something good. I want to ask you a question. Will you–

ZOE. *(overlapping)* Cut it out.

ADAM gets down on one knee, takes out a box.

ADAM. Will you–

ZOE. Adam I'm not kidding, cut it out, I don't want to hear it–

ADAM. Will you go to the Prom with me?

He opens the box. It's a gardenia corsage.

ZOE. *Fuck!* No!

ADAM. Has somebody asked you yet?!

ZOE. You've *got* somebody.

ADAM. That doesn't answer my question!

ZOE. You have somebody and so do I. Those are the rules.

ADAM. *Fuck the rules!*

ZOE. *We have an agreement!*

ADAM.	**ZOE.** *(simultaneous)*
We have a *history*! And history is more important than agreements! It can't continue to go on like it's been going on – I have too much in my heart, Zoe, I am too *full.* You haven't been invited to Prom yet so why are you telling me NO!	Don't start with that – I am so tired of your talk about history because history is what is PAST. It's OVER. It's DEAD. I am not going to get into this with you again – god we are not going to talk about the PROM!

ZOE. YOU KNOW WHY!

ADAM. SAY IT! SAY IT! TELL ME!

ZOE. *(overlap)* I DON'T HAVE TO TELL YOU ANYTHING!

The phone begins to ring. They stop. Pause.

ZOE *and* **ADAM** *rush for the phone and struggle for it.* **ADAM** *wins.*

ADAM. – Faculty Room.

– Oh you *do.* Right. Just a minute.

ZOE *grabs the phone and huddles in a corner to talk.*

ZOE. – Yes.

– Hi.

– Fine.

– No, I am. Really.

She gets that gooey soft look girls get when they're making up after a fight.

ZOE. – I'm sorry too.

   – No, I am. No, I am. No, I am.

   – Baby...Really?!

[giggles]

   – Yes. *Yes.* Uh huh. Uh huh.

   – After seventh period.

   – You're a goofball. No you are. No you are. No you are.

[giggles]

   – Love you too.

Little silence.

ZOE. I can't go to the Prom with you.

ADAM. Right. Fine.

ZOE. I'm *sorry.*

ADAM. It's called the faculty room for a reason. Student calls are inappropriate.

ZOE. Tss. I think I can recall a time when you weren't so strict about the rules of the faculty room.

ADAM. Things change.

ZOE. I said the exact same thing to Carver earlier today.

She resumes making Valentines.

ADAM. *(quiet)* I miss you.

ZOE. "Things change."

ADAM. Well, things are gonna keep changing, Zoe, I can assure you of that.

   ADAM *exits.* **ZOE** *makes Valentines.*

   P.A. SYSTEM *clicks on.*

P.A. SYSTEM. *[sound of coffee percolating]*
   [sound of someone drinking coffee, then saying "ahhh!"]
   Study Hall will begin in five minutes.

ZOE. Principal Dennis?

P.A. SYSTEM. Hmm? Who's that?

ZOE. Zoe Bartholomhew in the Faculty Room, Principal Dennis.

P.A. SYSTEM. Well how the heck are you, Miss Bartholomhew.

ZOE. Pretty good.

I wanted to ask you a question–

You used to teach here, before you were principal...

P.A. SYSTEM. Oh, sure I did, absolutely...course that was, you know, before the *Civil War... (laughter)*

ZOE. *(laughter)*

P.A. SYSTEM. Ha, ha ha.

ZOE. Do you, um, remember me as a student?

P.A. SYSTEM. Sure I do, Sure I do.

Pause.

P.A. SYSTEM. Was there anything else, Miss Bartholomew?

ZOE. I just wanted to know if teaching ever

Well did teaching ever–

Does teaching high school – and you know, Madison-Feurey's sort of off the main drag–

And, and kind of isolated – did teaching ever make you feel lonely?

Little pause.

Because sometimes I think – I believe that people here, basically want to be lifted up, at least I know that I want to feel more, more–

And you need help to get there, it's not something you can do all by yourself–

Do you understand what I mean?

Principal Dennis?

Sir?

Silence.

Blackout.

Scene Seven

MARCH

*A banner has been hung. It reads: **SPIRIT DAYS 5 4 3 2 1**. The **5 4 3** and **2** all have been X'd out.*

Sound of a light rain.

ZOE *and* **CARVER** *enter.* **ZOE** *holds a dog-eared manuscipt.*

CARVER. ...No, don't read to me. Just stop.

ZOE. Okay.

Little pause.

ZOE. Sorry, I have to.

Reading dramatically.

"Oh Craver, Craver, when the fire comes, you'll understand the Wrath of the Lamb."
Then the character wearing the stag's head enters. Sound of thunder. Then Darby says, *"Craver, when the rain comes, everything will change."* Then someone smites a prison guard. Then *you* say, *"Am I awake?"* Then–

CARVER. Cut it out!

He grabs the manuscript of the "play."

ZOE. It's pretty funny that your character's name is "Craver."

CARVER. It doesn't mean it's me.

ZOE. Carver, Craver. It's an anagram of your name, it's very clever.

CARVER. Darby's been writing this? For how long?

ZOE. A few weeks, I don't know.

CARVER. You and Adam knew all this time. When were you going to tell me?

ZOE. I am telling you.

CARVER. This "play..."

ZOE. *(correcting)* Ritual.

CARVER. Whatever. It's incredibly disturbing.

He flips through pages.

CARVER. It's *violent.* They think they're going to perform this? When?

ZOE. I guess…today.

CARVER. *(horrified)* At the rally?

ZOE. Adam gave Darby and the Book Club permission.

CARVER. That is not his call! Spirit Days is mine!

ZOE. They're rehearsing it outside right now.

> **ZOE** *and* **CARVER** *listen. Outside, from far off, we can hear a large group of students singing. This singing will be intermittently and* very faintly *audible throughout the rest of this scene.*
>
> *The words are not really intelligible. The singing should sound like monks chanting – formal, harmonious, but not as uplifting/dynamic as gospel music.*

CARVER. Everyone wants to sabotage my plans! First Mrs. Lund, now you!

ZOE. Oh, Craver. "When the rain –"

CARVER. Don't.

> **CARVER** *gets on the phone.*

CARVER. – Melanie, can you pull the class schedule for Darby Weider?

– Yeah. She's Adam's advisee.

– I want to know where she is right now.	**ZOE.** *(simultaneously)* I told you they're
– She has a free period?	rehearsing
– Where is she next period then.	on the quad. You can hear them.

– Okay. Thanks.

He hangs up.

ZOE's *cell rings – she's received a text message. She reads it, smiles. She texts a message, sends. Her cell rings again. She reads a message. She laughs.*

ZOE. What.

CARVER. I give up. Clearly it's more relaxing wherever you are. The place you live, in the Land of Lost Judgment.

ZOE. I live in heaven.

CARVER. You are so...flip. I'm tired of feeling *outraged* all the time. They're chanting for the ritual out there and you don't care because...never mind. Do you know how exhausting all this is? I used to play chess. I used to go antiquing. Now all I can do is breathe. That's my hobby. I took this job for a reason, breathe in, I'm here for a reason, breathe out. I just want Spirit Days to be – *oh my god*.

...because **ZOE** *has pushed up her sleeves to reveal her long scars; he's noticed them.*

ZOE. – Don't be weird.

CARVER *holds her arm outstretched, examines it. He takes an audible deep breath.*

CARVER. Tell me something. If you "live in heaven" ...why do you need to do this?

ZOE. I don't "need" to.

– I'm happy.

You know I'm trying to do my best.

ADAM *bangs open the door. He's flying on ecstasy.*

ADAM. I feel like something wonderful is going to happen. I feel lighter than smoke. This cigarette tastes sublime. You should see how well rehearsal's going out there, my friends, it's going to put the "It" back into Spirit Days.

CARVER. Well I have no idea how you think this "ritual" fits into Spirit Days. Thanks a lot!

[thunder]

ADAM. Oh, Darby wanted to keep it a surprise. Come on, it's an utterly colorless day and the students are making Art. I say Bravo.

Can I touch your hair?

Little pause.

ADAM. I don't *have* to touch your hair. It just looked soft in this glorious flourescent light. It's cool. It's all cool cool cool. Coooool. May I tell you something personal?

CARVER. Okay…

ADAM. This is important. I'm concerned that you may not listen to me, and that's okay. I'd prefer that you did listen to me, but I'm also going to love you just the same if you don't. Here's the thing: Jen Carlson is not really my girlfriend. That is to say, I give Jen a ride home on some afternoons, and I have on occasion kept her after school doing various useless activities, and I do believe that her peaches-and-cream complexion is the eighth wonder of the world…but she is not…technically…my girlfriend. I have not known her *biblically*. I haven't kissed her, I haven't copped a feel, I haven't gotten a blowjob, I haven't even touched her skin. I may have placed a hand on her shoulder, but if it happened, it was inadvertent. It's a charade. But I've led Zoe to believe that Jen is my girlfriend. I've led Zoe to believe that I've had many Madison-Feurey High girlfriends, but none of it has been true.

*The singing from outside begins to change. There is still singing, but there is also shouting. The sound of glass breaking. A low hum, almost inaudible. The sound of unrest. **CARVER** hears it. Sort of.*

Something wonderful is going to happen, and soon. Have you ever felt that way? It's in the air. Rain. An early spring. You think that's possible?

ZOE. No.

CARVER. Adam. You seem…

ADAM. I'm wonderful.

I just wanted to tell you something personal. Something true.

*He pats **CARVER**'s head.*

ZOE. Liar.

ADAM. I was lying *before*, Zoe, don't miss the point of my revelation.

Let's not talk about this any more – I've told you what I wanted to tell you. And it makes me feel warmly towards you both. Not in a sexual way.

CARVER. Fine. I mean–

ZOE. Carver let it be.

ADAM. I scored E from Loren Elliot.

CARVER. Oh, great.

ADAM. Zoe, you were right about Glenn, he *was* ripping me off. But Loren gave me a really good deal, and he is a wonderful, wonderful kid. Just a very special person, you know?

Sound from outside: the singing grows louder. More people have joined. There is clapping. More shouting.

ADAM. Loren and I took E together, and it was magnificent! It feels so good to be with both of you right now. Zoe, you're glowing, you know that? You're looking very healthy, very robust – actually you look fat.

CARVER. Adam–

ADAM. Shh it's okay, Carver, let's be honest, she looks *fat* – you look fat, but in a good way. Still pretty.

ZOE. Your girlfriend smells. Bad.

ADAM. I don't think you were listening: Jen Carlson is *not* my girlfriend–

[thunder, rain.]

ZOE. *(tightly)* Whoever she is, you should have a talk with her because she smells *terrible* and the other kids are talking about her. She needs a bath.

ADAM. She smells because she's throwing up her breakfast and her lunch in the bathroom stalls and it's hard to lose that smell. She's trying to get very, very thin. She's trying to make herself disappear. You know why? Because she loves this boy in her class and *HE'S FUCKING HER TEACHER*. She thinks that if she gets thinner, maybe he'll love her again.

ZOE. Well someone should tell her that losing weight that way isn't an answer.

ADAM. Yeah, look at *you*! I mean, that's what Raphael likes, right? *Fat!*

CARVER. Both of you: *stop!* Would you *listen* to yourselves!

ADAM. I am listening. I feel like something wonderful could happen, I really do. I can see the Rapture from here, and it is so beautiful.

ZOE. After you've talked for *years* about Beth Fisher, Chrissy Cornwall, Samantha Prado, Stephie Sommers, the "experiment" with Sterling Mills – you are full of shit, sweetheart.

I am inside of something so pure you can't even see it. I have waited my whole life to be loved like this. Raphael Gilberto is who I was made for. Every weekend all I do is eat. Pringles, Hershey's Kisses, Ben & Jerry's, Domino's double crust. All I do is watch movies where things explode. All I do is listen to music that splits my head wide open. All I do is touch his skin, the most perfect skin, unblemished, clean, with a smell like – like nothing else. He's not my boyfriend. He's *me*. We're soul mates. He is *why I exist*. Get it.

BILL enters holding a pistol from Morning Checkpoints.
ADAM grabs BILL by the shoulders.

ADAM. Bill! If I gave you a knife, would you cut my head open? Maybe not a knife, a machete. Yes: a single cut. If my head were opened up, something wonderful could spring out. Something glorious. A daughter. That's how Zeus had Athena. Goddess of wisdom. He had a headache, they sliced his head open, and out she flew. You think you could try something like that with me? Whadda you say.

ADAM takes a marker and draws a dotted line across his forehead.

ADAM. Right here.

BILL just stands there.

ADAM. Blah, blah, blah, Bill, give someone else a word.

ADAM *grabs the pistol from* **BILL,** *opens chamber.*

ADAM. *Someone* was careless about ammo check! One left over!

He spins the chamber, places the barrel under his chin.

ADAM. God, I feel *wonderful.*

He pulls the trigger. Click. He looks at the gun.

ADAM. My only wish is that the Rapture would hurry the fuck up, because I'm not at all tired. I'm awake. I am as alert as a goddamn soldier.

Bell rings.

Everyone freezes, listening.

The sound of rain begins.

The bell continues to ring.

Scene Eight

ONE HOUR LATER

Rain outside.

ADAM *and* **CARVER** *race into the faculty room.*

They're soaked.

Intermittent warning bells.

Cacophony outside the faculty room. A mob of students running through the hall, banging on lockers, breaking glass, whooping.

Most importantly, there is the sound of a group of students singing. It sounds like a larger group than the previous scene, and the singing should be stronger. The singing remains otherworldly – harmonious, but also unfamiliar.

A voice through a megaphone in the distance:

MEGAPHONE VOICE. *(very distorted)* If you are currently in the main building, you must remain indoors until we are able to secure the premises. remain indoors. Do not, I repeat, do not leave the building to go outside.

The **P.A. SYSTEM** *clicks on.*

P.A. SYSTEM. *[static]*

> **CARVER** *stands close to the* **P.A. SYSTEM** *and shouts into it.*

CARVER. Hello? Principal Dennis, HELLO!?

GIRL'S VOICE OVER THE P.A. SYSTEM. Miss Bartholemhew?

CARVER. Who's that? – Hello?

ADAM. Jen? Is that you? *(to* **CARVER***)* It's Jen Carlson.

CARVER. Jennifer!

> *[static]*

> **P.A. SYSTEM** *clicks off.*

CARVER. Goddammit.

ADAM. Someone said Danny Persitch attacked Coach Salata.

CARVER. Someone said Norah Blakey sacrificed a lamb.

ADAM. *(overlapping)* Someone said Christina Harrison set a school bus on fire.

Another horde runs though the hallway outside, hammering on the faculty room door, but the door doesn't open and they keep running until another door slams.

CARVER *begins moving furniture against the door as a barricade.*

CARVER. Okay Adam HELP me!

ADAM. You think that's going to make a difference?

CARVER. YES. I DO. AND I NEED YOU TO HELP.

Sound of lightning outside. **ADAM** *helps* **CARVER** *move furniture.*

ADAM. Carver. What if everybody is awake already?

CARVER. JUST FOCUS AND MOVE THE COUCH.

ADAM. What if the Rapture happened before we were born. What if it happened a long time ago and everybody forgot?

[sound of a helicopter]

ADAM. Maybe it doesn't matter whether we're *awake.* Or *not.*

You just have to *do* Good. And the problem is: what's Good?

The barricade is complete.

CARVER. You – You do your best.

ADAM. But what if your "best" isn't *Good*? But it's still your best?

The phone rings. **CARVER** *runs for it.*

CARVER. – Yes! Hello!

– Darby!

It's Darby.

– I don't know what that means.

CARVER. – I can't.

> – If you're going to *chant*, I can't help you.

> – Darby, this not a healthy way to achieve your goals!

> *To* ADAM

> She's speaking in tongues. I think it's tongues.
> *An otherworldly sound over the phone.*
> *Outside: a shot.* CARVER *and* ADAM *react.*

> *Banging on the door.*

CARVER. YOU STAY OUT! GO AWAY! YOU HAVE NO BUSINESS HERE!

ZOE. *(outside door)* DAMMIT CARVER IT'S ME! OPEN THE DOOR!

>> ADAM *helps* CARVER *move the couch somewhat away from the door.* ZOE *enters, climbing over/past the couch.* ZOE *is also very wet.*

ZOE. Where's Raphael?

> I texted him to come here.

> *Singing outside, along with the sounds of chaos. Another gunshot.*

>> ZOE *texts and tries to send, unsuccessfully.*

ZOE. Fuck.

CARVER. *(deeply upset)* Are they shooting? Why are they shooting?

ADAM. Something powerful is happening that they don't understand.

CARVER. *(turning on him)* What is it they don't understand, Adam? The *ritual. Lightning! Chanting!* Do *you* understand that?!

ADAM. Maybe.

ZOE. *(to* ADAM*)* You did this.

ADAM. Carver's in charge of Spirit Days!

ZOE. It's *your* book club. Darby got everyone worked up.

CARVER. *(listening)* The singing…it isn't – English. Is it?

> *More singing. Another gunshot. Shouting. The singing continues.*

CARVER. We confiscate every weapon, every day. There's a *system.* No one's going to…

ADAM. Jen Carlson had a gun.

CARVER. You didn't take it from her?

ADAM. She said…it was a prop for the play.

ZOE. There are a lot of police out there.

ADAM. *(to* **CARVER***)* Darby was pointing at you.

CARVER. FUCK YOU! AND FUCK YOUR BOOK CLUB!

ADAM. I thought everything we read would have prepared me for this. I thought I'd be ready.

CARVER. Those are police, not *angels.*

ADAM. You sure?

ZOE. *(to* **ADAM***)* Why didn't you tell them to stop.

CARVER. *(to* **ADAM***) Why* was Darby pointing at me?

The phone rings.

ADAM. Because you're the sign?

CARVER. The sign of what.

ZOE *picks it up.*

ZOE. Hello who is this. *Hello.*

She taps the hang up button in frustration.

ZOE. Is that you? Raphael?

She slams the phone down.

CARVER. Are we – in danger?

ADAM. We're sleeping.

[thunder]

ZOE. *(shaken, near tears)* I saw Jen Carlson. She was in the middle of everything, next to Darby, singing. I was looking for Raphael, and Jen saw me. She looked at me so strangely.

Little pause.

She's really thin.

The faraway chanting/singing grows louder.

CARVER. No one's coming to help us.

[Sound of GIANT thunder crack, rain.]

The lights flicker; quite a few go out. Emergency lighting. The singing fades.

ADAM. This is like campfire girls.

CARVER. Shut *up!*

More rain.

ADAM. Zoe and I got married on a rainy Thursday afternoon just like this one. And the next day she still turned in her homework on time.

Little pause.

CARVER. What did you just say.

ADAM. I kept all her papers. Still have 'em.

CARVER. Tell me what you just said.

ADAM. I wanted to wait. I wanted to wait and I couldn't because, because, I don't know why. It was stupid – it was *idiotic* but it *wasn't*, because I loved her.

ZOE. He did. And I knew it.

CARVER. *(to* **ZOE***)* You were his student.

ZOE. Yes.

ADAM. She walked into my homeroom and she said: "I know you love me."

ZOE. I was fifteen.

ADAM. My heart stopped. I couldn't breathe.

CARVER. *(to* **ADAM***)* You were her teacher.

ZOE. When I looked at him I *knew*. This, this was love.

ADAM. In that moment, I believed in god, I was the infidel who became a believer.

[thunder]

ZOE. He *saw* me. He looked at me like birds were going to fly out of my hair. I'm supposed to say "no" to that love? What would "no" get me? Nothing. I said: *yes*.

ADAM. What did I tell you.

ZOE. You said I was going to break your heart. You said that was how it worked.

ADAM. I said that. I'm pretty smart. I'm pretty stupid.

ZOE. I don't love you anymore.

Voices through a megaphone; a helicopter; breaking glass.

ADAM. *(to* **ZOE***)* I know.

ZOE. I'm sorry.

ADAM. I know.

Ah, fuck. My head feels so strange. There was this long burst of color and clarity and I understood everything and I liked everybody and I believed in God.

I want to be Awake.

Glass breaking in the distance; shouting; singing.

ZOE*'s cell goes off: a text message. She reads it.*

ZOE. Goddamit.

ADAM. How come you're crying.

ZOE. Raphael can't get in. I don't know why. He's in the gym and he can't get here.

ADAM. Zoe. I'll find him. I can do that. I'll go outside and get him. Okay?

ZOE. I love him.

ADAM. I know.

I'll bring him to you. That's good, a good thing, right?

ADAM *exits.*

ZOE. I tried to stop loving him. Raphael. I did try.

I would wake up in the morning and I would say, okay. Make today "normal." I would eat a piece of toast. I would drink a cup of tea. I would drive at the exact speed limit all the way to school and I would park at the far end of the lot. And when I walked into my classroom, there he was. No matter how early I came, he was always there. I'd begin a lesson and my own voice would sound too loud in my ears. I was on fire, you couldn't stop me. And of course that was because I was teaching for him. I was myself. My best self.

I know you think I'm... sick.

CARVER. You don't know what I think.

Singing, voices through a megaphone.

ZOE. I should have told you before. About me and Adam.
I just – it *upset* me when you wouldn't admit what had
happened at your old school.

CARVER. *Nothing happened.*

Little pause.

ZOE. BULLSHIT, CARVER! DON'T YOU DARE GET
HOLIER THAN THOU. YOU WERE IN LOVE. WITH
YOUR STUDENT. FUCK YOU FOR PRETENDING!

CARVER. *Love* him?! Love Sam?! He was an *annoyance.* He
jeopardized my – everything. He fucked up my career.

[thunder crack]

I wanted to do good things, really good things. Then:
the letters. The unceasing letters. Messages on chalk
boards. All about me. I had to erase the board at the
beginning of every class, every day. I called his parents.
I filed a report with the district. The response? I should
be able to *handle* a "crush."

So. I met with Sam. He brought me roses.

I told him that his behavior was inappropriate. I said
he was in danger of being expelled. Sam said fine,
great, perfect: then we could be together. He tried to
kiss me. He said we were "soul mates." And something
rose up in me.

And I said:

"Sam. This all has to stop.

I don't love you.

I don't *like* you.

You don't matter to me. You don't matter."

And Sam – backed away. He said "okay." He walked
out and I breathed a sign of relief. I did it! I would
have my classroom back. I would have my life back.
Later that night, he bought gasoline and…you know
the rest.

I wasn't afraid to love him. I really didn't. Love him.
I was his teacher, and I showed exactly how much I
cared. Not at all.

Emergency lights flicker up – the regular lights return.

The door begins to open.

ZOE. WHO'S THERE!

In walks **BILL**. *He carries an umbrella. He is not wet.*

He shakes the water off the umbrella and closes it.

BILL. I believe you should know about the event I witnessed a moment ago. I was standing beside the statue of Dolly Madison. From my vantage point, I saw our colleague Mr. Younger on the roof of the gym. His arms were outstretched. It looked rather like a painting. The police were distressed to see him up there: they called to him repeatedly through a megaphone. Mr. Younger gave no indication that he heard them. He seemed to be searching the sky. Then there was a flash of lightning, very close – it may have struck a tree across the street. The brightness of it caused me to shield my eyes. When I looked up again, Mr. Younger was gone.

CARVER. He…fell. He was *struck*, and he fell.

BILL. No.

CARVER. What do you mean "no."

ZOE. He was shot.

BILL. There was no body. Not on the roof, not on the ground. One moment he was looking into the sky. The next moment, wshhh.

CARVER. Adam…*disappeared*?

ZOE. People don't disappear.

BILL. I thought that, as well. Nonetheless. I saw what I saw.

Little pause.

BILL. Excuse me.

BILL *goes to the phone, dials.*

BILL. Principal Dennis. Bill Dunn here.
    – Because I don't *want* to use the P.A. System, Robert.
    – I'm calling to tender my resignation.
    – Effective immediately.

BILL. – Well – because I saw a miracle.

– You too, Robert. My best to Karen.

BILL hangs up.

ZOE. Bill. You...*talk.*

BILL. When I have something to say.

He readies himself to exit.

BILL. Time to go home.

I think you both should stay in here for the time being.
An officer was struggling with a student outside.

ZOE. What student? Who?

BILL. Jen Carlson.

BILL exits.

ZOE and CARVER sit in silence. Then ZOE stands.

ZOE. Maybe I can help.

*ZOE goes to the door, opens it, and steps into the hall.
From the end of the hall, we hear another door open.*

ZOE. ...Jen?

BLAM.

CARVER reacts, ducking, or dropping to the ground.

In the hall, ZOE crumples and falls. Blood.

A moment of total quiet.

CARVER raises his head and sees ZOE on the ground.

Blackout.

In the dark, an ambulance siren.

Scene Nine

SOME TIME LATER

CARVER *sits at the table, pale. He holds an unlit ciga-*
rette.

The school is eerily silent.

A knock at the door. Slowly, it's pushed open. A STU-
DENT *stands in the door, unsure of what to do. Judging*
from the STUDENT*'s size and demeanor, he's in ninth*
grade.

STUDENT. Mr. Durand? Hey.

Wow. I've never been in here before. I always wondered
what it looked like. "The Inner Sanctum." Ha ha.

CARVER *doesn't respond.*

The STUDENT *moves tentatively around, checking*
things out.

STUDENT. I mean…you know, the faculty room. "Oooh,
don't go in there." Ha ha.

There are, um, you know, some people out there. Looking for you. You probably know that. I just thought I'd,
ah, come in and tell you.

CARVER. Thank you. *(with some effort)* What grade are you
in?

STUDENT. Uh, I'm a freshman.

A little awed.

There's camera crews out there and everything.

CARVER. You're not in my homeroom.

STUDENT. Uh no, I have Mrs. Lund.

She was telling everybody to line up, and then she
wasn't there anymore. Same with Jason Park and Tina
Kring and Kerry Sullivan. Weird, huh?

The STUDENT *spies the giant Cardinal head.*

STUDENT. Oh my god, that *head* is still here...I remember that mascot from when my brother went to school here, and he graduated, like, a *long* time ago. Man. Why would you guys even keep that thing?

Realizing.

Wow, it is really, seriously ugly in here. I mean *ugly*.

CARVER. That's true. It is.

STUDENT. You guys need some light in here. It's ridiculous.

CARVER *has begun to cry. The* STUDENT *notices.*

STUDENT. Oh, oh, hey, I didn't mean to – I mean, it's ugly, but it can be fixed, probably. Don't worry, Mr. Durand. I mean, it's bad in here, but it isn't your fault. Right? I mean you can't have light with no windows. It's not your fault.

CARVER. Mrs. Lund is gone?

STUDENT. Maybe she'll come back.

CARVER *keeps crying, his face in his hands. The* STUDENT *approaches him.*

STUDENT. It's okay, Mr. Durand.

Standing behind CARVER, *the* STUDENT *places a hand on his shoulder as he cries.*

STUDENT. Everything is going to be okay.

P.A. SYSTEM. *[flapping of wings]*

End of Play

PROP LIST

Scene One
Papers to grade
Pile of books, incl. "365 Meditations for Teachers"
Zoe's "Once-chic" bag
Cigarettes
3 or 4 handguns
Coffee cups
Pack of Marlboros
Briefcase with a personal mug inside

Scene Two
Ghost costume
Keyboard, headphones
Witch costume
Handgun and rifle
Priest costume, incl. rosary
"Sudden Awakening" Novel
Cigarette, lighter
Bowl of candy corn
Tambourine, box of music

Scene Three
Stapler
Paper leaves
Fabric
Papers to grade
Marijuana pipe, lighter
Comb
Coats
Flask

Scene Four
Sock puppets with googly eyes
Gloves
Gun
Purse
Big pink paper flower (boutonniere)
Exacto knife

Scene Five
Book club flyer
Snow
Papers
Folded origami note
Headphones, player
Twinkie
Plastic knife
Fritos
Cokes
Zoe's bag
Ding Dongs, bags of chips
Briefcase
"Wake Up" sign

Scene Six
Carver's lunch
Zoe's lunch, Sno-balls
Milk
Construction paper
Doilies
Glue
Exacto knife
Box with gardenia corsage

Scene Seven
Banner: "SPIRIT DAYS 5-4-3-2-1" with X's over "5," "4," "3," and "2,"
Manuscript
Zoe's cell phone
Cigarette
Pistol
Marker

Scene Eight
Zoe's phone
Umbrella (wet)

Scene Nine
Unlit cigarette